W9-BAW-160

MY ROMANCE

ALSO BY GORDON LISH

Dear Mr. Capote

What I Know So Far

Peru

Mourner at the Door

Extravaganza

MY ROMANCE

A Novel

Gordon Lish

W. W. NORTON & COMPANY
NEW YORK · LONDON

PRINTED IN THE UNITED STATES OF AMERICA.
THE TEXT OF THIS BOOK IS COMPOSED IN BEMBO
WITH THE DISPLAY SET IN KAP-ANTIQUA STANDARD.
COMPOSITION AND MANUFACTURING BY
THE HADDON CRAFTSMEN, INC.
BOOK DESIGN BY CHARLOTTE STAUB.
FIRST EDITION

LIBRARY OF CONGRESS CATALOGING-IN-PUBLICATION DATA

LISH, GORDON.
MY ROMANCE : A NOVEL / GORDON LISH.
P. CM.
I. TITLE.
PS3562.I74M9 1991
813'.54—DC20 90-24142

ISBN 0-393-03001-6

W.W. NORTON & COMPANY, INC.
500 FIFTH AVENUE, NEW YORK, N.Y. 10110
W.W. NORTON & COMPANY, LTD.
10 COPTIC STREET, LONDON WC1A 1PU

1 2 3 4 5 6 7 8 9 0

FOR BARBARRA, BELOVED WIFE,

AND TO DON DELILLO II

He answers:

"By the order of the questions."

—EDMOND JABÈS

RAIN, RAIN,

GO AWAY,

COME AGAIN

ANOTHER DAY.

MY ROMANCE

What a difficulty it must be for us all that it was destined to be such a long and, as you can now hear, applauseless walk for me to make it up here to here at the lectern from where I had been sitting next to Jim Salter. Well, the distance was too great for show business's sake, and I was slowed by all the books you can see that I have carried on up here with me. Truth to tell, I do not know yet if I will in fact be reading from any one of them—although I certainly know why this one was one of the ones I thought to bring on up here with me. Oh, no, it was never to read from it but instead just to exhibit it to you before I give it to Bill Roberson as the handiest token of my gratitude to him for his inviting me out here to his Long Island University writers' conference, I suppose it is called, summer after summer. As you can see, it is Q14, or, more formally, the fourteenth number of *The Quarterly,* which is the literary magazine I put out, this with the spacious backing of Random House. Anyway, I want for you to see this sample of the latest number of the magazine and to maybe feel yourselves under urgent orders to go out and buy yourselves your own wonderful copy of same before I hand off this specimen of it to Bill Roberson in small answer to his many great courtesies to me before I made my walk up here this evening. Speaking of which, I must offer the observation that tonight, for the first time in all the summers that I have been coming out here to Southampton to read in the evening and then to teach in the morning, I must, I think, tell you that tonight I actually made an effort to solicit whiskey out there in the lobby prior to my making my long walk up here. Indeed, it is, so far as I can remember, or would be maybe willing to admit, the first time in as many as seven years that I have asked anybody anywhere for a drink. You see, I used to put away as much as a bottle and a half a day, sometimes probably even as much as two bottles a day, an amount, by the way, it pleases me, I suppose, to report to you, given that I am such a small man, as you can see, that I am not a large man, as you can certainly see, and that this kind of consumption of whiskey was obviously getting it down and keeping it down on a pretty bigtime scale. But stopped doing this, I stopped drinking like this—stopped swallowing whiskey at all, in fact—in 1983, I think it was. Almost positive that that was the year when I stopped doing it, the recollection of dates being not a feat I was ever very good at, as my grammar-school teachers would never have any trouble noticing and remembering. Oh, may have had one glass somewhere there in the seven years. Cannot say when—but can say that it was definitely with Denis Donoghue, a detail I am probably remembering because of Donoghue's size, he being such a large man, such a very large man, surely an immense man in any kind of comparison with the likes of me. Well, yes, yes—it was just after a night of stupefying nonsense mounted down at New York University, some sort of hideous literary logrolling staged down there at N.Y.U. Anyway, it was right after it was over that Donoghue and my wife Barbara and I went in flight to a nearby watering hole. Yes, yes, One Fifth Avenue it was, where I went ahead and did what I ought not to have done, had a glass, had a whole glass, in fact, either of Metaxa or of J.T.S. Brown. No, no, it wasn't of Metaxa, it was not of Metaxa, because I remember that the waiter said no, no, there was not any Metaxa. So I had to have what I liked—and would still like, I suppose, much less well—namely, a bourbon that goes by the name J.T.S. Brown. A glass right up to the very tippy-top of it, given that I was, and am, always in such a lather to keep up with Donoghue's colossally greater size and mind. It broke Barbara's heart, I think. To see it, to see me sitting there drinking this whole tumbler of straight whiskey—I bet it just broke her heart, to see me breaking the good behavior that I had set into place in 1983, I think the year was. But it had been a terrible night for all of us and it was Denis who was with us, and I think Barbara was willing to be abiding on the outside, anyhow, Donoghue's distinguished presence construing a sort of permission for exception maybe, his exception facilitating another exception. But getting back to tonight, that night with Donoghue was, I swear it, the sole exception in seven years. Until, that is, tonight, that is. Oh, but make no mistake of it, I did not get any whiskey down into me before my coming up here. Not that I did not try to. I mean, ask for it. Out there in the lobby before we all came in here into the auditorium, I was asking people for it—for a drink, for some whiskey, for some liquor—absolutely any species of it. I mean, I admit it, I was looking for something to help me get my courage up, to help me get my voice up—because I was feeling as if my voice was dying into a certain hoarseness and that, even if you could hear me all right, even if it would be possible for you to hear me all right, that my voice, it would sound small and weak and negligible. So I asked some people I thought would have something, who I thought might be carrying something with them—Salter and Madison Smartt Bell, Bill Tester, Bill Roberson, Star Sandow—a bottle, like one of those little tenths I used to keep in these big pockets I have. A pint, a half-pint, a flask—something. But I have to tell you that nobody had anything—not Salter, not Bell, not Tester and the rest—Alper, I asked Eleanor Alper, and Konrad, I asked Evelyn Konrad even—and even the young man out there—Jesus, I cannot believe this—I actually even asked the young man whom you all saw sitting out there at the ticket table who was selling the softcover edition of *Peru.* Jesus. Ah, but, as I said, nobody had anything—or anyway, nobody was telling me they had anything. So that here I am, standing up here now, sober as a judge now—and hearing my voice sound so small to me, so grimly weak, so entirely eviscerated to me. But, listen, I should be glad. That there was nobody who said to me, "Yeah, sure, Gordon—here, take a taste of this," I really should be very glad that there was nobody who said anything like this. Because, look, it was never just because I was drinking so much that it made sense for me to stop. It was not breaking Barbara's heart to see me break my non-batting streak that night with Donoghue just because she was seeing me drink so much. No, no, the fact is that I am not supposed to be drinking any alcohol at all, but not because of the notion of my being, let us say, a drunk or anything. No, no, the big thing about my drinking or, all right, about my not drinking, it has actually and solely—okay, chiefly, then—let us just say chiefly, then—to do with a certain medication I have to take. Namely, methotrexate. It goes by the name of methotrexate, this substance that I have to take to help try to keep—here comes yet another exasperatingly tricky customer to get pronounced clearly enough for you to hear it through this microphone I have up here—psoriasis—to help try to keep my psoriasis under control. Metaxa, methotrexate, psoriasis—ah, God, these words of my life. Well, the point is this—this methotrexate that I have to take, it irritates, if this is the word—well, it bothers the liver. Hence, why it is not at all good sense for me to drink, and why I was wise to stop, and why it was the best of luck for me that it proved that there was no one who was going to reach into his pocket or handbag and cooperate with me out there in the lobby tonight. You see, taking methotrexate for the psoriasis I have, this is a practice that pesters the liver just as much as it is reasonable for anyone to pester it—whereas going ahead and adding whiskey to one's diet, that's insult, I suppose you could say. So, okay, all thanks to Salter and so forth, to Bell and Tester and Sandow and Konrad and Alper and Roberson and so on, that everybody said no dice. Because this psoriasis that I have, it has been in a pretty bad way of late, given some trials that have lately been going on in my life. So there is absolutely no question but that I am probably going to be needing all the methotrexate I am going to be able to get into myself in the months coming up. God knows that one thing which I do not want to hear is the doctor saying to me, "Gordon, that's it, your liver's so bad you can't have any more of the stuff." On the other hand, it's not that methotrexate is the only substance I am standing here depending on to keep me from having lesions all over me until I am nothing but one big lesion again. Because that is exactly, in case you want to know, what the psoriasis has once or twice in my life finally sat down and made up its mind to do to me—namely, cover me all up completely. No, no, the fact is that there is another meth-sounding material that keeps me from having the worst happen to me—which in this case is called methoxsalen, and which is not to be confused with Metaxa or with methotrexate, of course. Great Jesus, I have to tell you how it has made me feel stronger up here, even larger up here—just to say, after all these years of my being so much in its company—to say Metaxa. Oh, just to say the word. Or is it name? Not word but name? Well, methoxsalen's no hardship on the liver, I don't think. I mean, nobody, no physician, has yet to say to me that it is. On the other hand, neither is it the great boon to me that methotrexate is. Still, it does work sort of a wonder, methoxsalen does. Methoxsalen definitely does contrive to create a sort of miracle for me, you might say. Heaven knows this is how I'd put it, a miracle, given the effect the methoxsalen can snatch from the sun—or anyhow from the ultraviolet light in the energy that comes to us from the sun. Well, I need all the help I can get. Now more than ever I can certainly see that I need all the help I can get—these meth-sounding substances. Because things are happening in my life, you see. There is something that has been lately happening in my life, you see—and it is clear to me—my God, is it ever clear to me—that I am going to have to have not just my psoriasis under control but everything else in reach for me to be able to manage what this thing that has newly been happening in my life is going to expect of me, or exact from me. I mean, there is no choice. I am going to have to be the best I have ever been able to be if I am ever going to be able to do my part with this thing. Listen, if there was anything on my mind this afternoon, this in the course of my bus ride out here from New York to Long Island this afternoon, it was that now is the time for me to start getting to be as big and as strong as I can possibly be. Because, as I said, and as is true, what other choice is there for me? There is no choice, you see. I mean, it was when I was there on the bus—it is such a long ride out to Southampton on the bus—it was all those awful miles that I was sitting there and just beginning to really feel—I mean, in my legs, in my back, in my arms—what it is really going to mean to me, this thing that is going to be expected of me, given the difficulty that has just suddenly come along and presented itself to me in my life just now. Do you understand what I mean when I say to you that I could feel it, that I could feel the meaning of it, in these arms of mine, in these hands, which you can sit there and see up here? These legs, this back, this meager body—it's all, it is all there is for me to manage with. Because my mind and my heart, they are going to be only partially the issue. Which is why that I do not think that I am actually going to be reading to you from any of these books that I walked up here with. Yes, yes, you, if you were listening, might have heard Bill Roberson citing certain ones of these very books that are up here at the lectern with me when he spoke to you about me when he himself was standing up here at the lectern and, what do they call it, introducing me. The point is, I suddenly feel it would be just proving to myself all the weakness that is in me if I were to just go ahead and do the usual thing, just proceed as expected in the customary manner—namely, to just stand up here and read to you from this or that page of the various writings I have been willing to live with to date. No, no, no, no, I have to tell you, standing up here now, even back when I was sitting back there on the bus, even then, it has been occurring to me with more and more panic that I just cannot go on and do what I have been doing, that there is no choice for me but to go ahead and make myself do something different—something as different as I can make myself do—if only to honor, in an outward way, some of the exorbitance that has been going on with me in an inward way ever since this thing came into my life. Into my wife's life actually, into Barbara's life actually. I am desperate standing up here. I feel a certain desperation standing up here. I do not want just to stand up here and read stories to you. It is not good enough for me to just stand up here and do my best to read to you from up here. I want instead to speak to you from up here. I just feel that I have to speak to you from up here. I mean, I did not know that my life was ever going to get to be like this. My God, I used to think, it was only until very recently that I used to think, that my life had already been as dramatic as it was ever going to get. Jesus, those times when I was a boy in insane asylums, those times when I was in Arizona playing at being a cowboy, those times of my running wild with Neal Cassady and with Ken Kesey, those times of my romance with Barbara, that time of my being fired from schoolteaching—Jesus, there was a time when I would have told you that these were the times of my life, that there would never be any more vehement times for me in my life. Wrong, wrong, wrong. As is, I suppose, to be expected with every unsuspecting one of us—wrong, wrong, wrong. Live long enough and I think you will see—wrong, wrong, wrong. As, for that matter, Kesey himself was so impossibly taught, this in the passing of his son Jed. Well, we learn to grapple, and think that we have had all the learning we will ever need to have—to grapple. Finally, with our death. But live long enough and life might deliver you to conditions for which you never imagined you would have been better to have had training. Take this evening. Take the bus ride that got me out to you here for this evening. Because just previous to it, to the long ride out here, I had had myself, as had Barbara, an even longer ride, a plane ride, back to New York from Switzerland. Where Barbara and I had gone to—along, of course, with our son Atticus—in order for us all to have—together, the three of us all together—one last family holiday. But I must tell you that for my part, and I am next to certain for Barbara and Atticus's, we never, for more than an instant here and there, outran the dread that had sent our little family on its mission. Immediately upon our return to New York, in the early evening just before the one before this one, what had propelled us on our way drove down upon our hearts with all the same old terror. Or anyhow down upon mine, I must say—since I am not competent to speak, with any exactitude at all, respecting the hearts of the other two parties. Oh, it was worse to come home. All those fabulously costly exertions—for I am such a miserly little bastard—and yet, even so, it was worse for us than I think it had been for us before we had even spent one dime. Or, wait a minute, wait a sec—Swiss franc, that is. One Swiss franc, that is. So you see, it is because of this—because of this ponderousness that slammed itself back down all around me even more utterly than ever two evenings ago—that I just know that I cannot let this event here go off according to routine model. Or, to put it the way I feel it, I just know that I have to do something different, something illegal, something pretty incommensurate, I think. I mean, I think I have to make a reply of some kind, produce a scream of some kind—shout back, you might say. Scare myself, change the terms, rearrange the rules, let recklessness overtake me, see if I can outrun habit, make a friend of chaos. So what I think I am going to do is not read from any of the books that I have laid down here on top of the lectern. What I am going to do, I think, is take them all off the top of the lectern and shift them all down to the little shelf that's down here down near the bottom of the lectern—and instead, if I can find it, take out the business card that I had put some notes on and then put into one of my pockets while I was sitting out there with you next to Salter listening to Bill Roberson introduce me. I mean, I know what I wrote, I am almost positive that I can recall what I wrote—I know it was four entries and a title, and I am next to certain that I could probably recite for you what they all were, the four entries and the title—okay, I am stalling, you can doubtless tell that I am standing here stalling—but as you can also probably see, or saw at least as I walked up here, my trousers are excessively large, I wear these trousers that are lavishly large, and it is sometimes no easy business, I can tell you, fetching anything back up from out of these pockets—sometimes to find something, to get your hand on something, you have to really reach around inside of these unusually large pockets. Did I tell you I used to slip tenths into these pockets?—and that nobody at Knopf—that is where I work, at the publishing house that is a division of Random House and that is known as Alfred A. Knopf, and then before that at *Esquire,* before I worked at Knopf I worked at the magazine known as *Esquire*—did I yet make the point this evening that I was able to get a tenth of whiskey into these pockets without anybody at Knopf or at *Esquire*—or so I like to think, at least—ever being any the wiser? Or pints or half-pints or whatever they were—because with trousers like these, you could really hide things—ah, here it is! Got it, got it! Down among the subway tokens and the felt-tips and the notes I am always making and sticking into my pockets, and all the loose change and my keys, this big bunch of keys—and there is this little container of mini-mints I always carry—Certs, that is. Habit, that is. All the years when it was crucial for me to disguise my otherwise telltale breath, you see. Oh, and you know what else I can feel down in there on this side? Because it is this lipstick sort of affair I have acquired from Barbara—you see, you see? To use to smear on over certain spots of psoriasis when they crop up on my hands and face when the prospect is that I am going to be going somewhere—seen, that is—you know, such as at the office, or, for example, up here on this stage, for example—where it would be good for me to tone them down a bit—namely, these new little lesions of psoriasis that are always cropping up on me with always a little too much vividness for me to handle it just at the start of it. Well, I am a vain man—this must be evident. At any rate, I've got it, I have got it—here it finally is—and, as you can see, it is my business card, it is one of the business cards Knopf has been, since 1976, printing up for me, *Gordon Lish, Editor,* and the rest of the pertinent particulars, all very prettily elevated from the surface of the paper—but over here on this side—look, you could not possibly determine this from where you are sitting, but over here on the other side, here are the four entries I told you that I made when I was sitting out there with Salter—and the title, down at the bottom, here is the title, which you cannot see, of course, but here it is, written down here at the bottom of my business card—namely *My Romance.* You cannot see it, but that's it, that is what it says, it says *My Romance*—whereas just above it, noted in just this sequence just above it, here are the four entries I awhile ago remarked—"The Watch," "The Oil," "The Crosley," "The Room," which last entry I think I really should have made not "The Room" but "The Office." But so be it, let it stand—I promised myself a walk with no net—to go back and make it "The Office" would be like going back to hold on for a while longer when it's now or never if you're ever going to make the walk. Well, look, these four jottings—five, really—that are on here on this business card here, I am going to make a certain use of them that will be like nothing I have ever done. Because, the way things are, the way I have been hinting at that things just suddenly for me and my family are, it is in my heart to feel that I must stand up here and do something, do anything, that I have never done before—so why not stand and talk it out, I'm saying, the four jottings bearing in on me as my vectors, as it were—or probably more as governance than as vectors, I guess—what I will go ahead and call a light novel? A small man's novel, a quick man's novel—but, no, not a novelette, not a novella, no, no. But a light novel, whatever a light novel might turn out in my mouth to be—my father and I, for example, sitting together with one another, sitting next to a swimming pool together with one another, sitting there in August across from one another, but the two of us parted by the light, of course. I mean, this discourse that I am going to embark on just as soon as I have rummaged around in these ramblings enough and turned up a sentence that sounds to me like the likeliest start, maybe it will sound something like a novel to you, even though it is going to get itself composed—well, concocted, at least—from talk as I talk. Oh, I don't doubt you will think this a trick of some sort—and you would be right in so thinking, I suppose. But how I am going to do the trick I cannot tell you, given that I have never done it before. On the other hand, it occurs to me to say that there is nothing that we do that is not a trick of some sort. Depend upon it—that if people do it, there must be a pretty good trick to it. Well, it is not the kind of trick I had in mind—but, yes, yes, there certainly is a trick to getting this watch off—or fastened. You see the kind of band it has? Well, the clasp is tricky to handle, no doubt about it. In any event, this watch you see up here on my wrist, this is the watch. Can you see the band from where you are? It is constituted of these little teeny tiny links. They're gold—white gold—as is, of course, the case itself. Anyway, I am going to take this wristwatch off, work this tricky clasp—both to show the wristwatch to you, on the one hand—and, too, to lay it down here on the lectern so that I might have it here right in front of me for me to check the time from time to time, again as governance, you understand, to try to keep myself on course. I mean, from time to time you might catch me looking down here at the lectern—but please know that I will be doing so only for civility's sake—namely, to see that I am, one, keeping my light-novelizing within the range of time Bill Roberson has allotted to me—and, two, to remind myself to keep sticking to my categories and to encourage any overlappings that might be construed from them—they being, these categories, I hope you have not already let yourself forget, "The Watch," "The Oil," "The Crosley," and—too bad, bad luck—not "The Office" but "The Room." At any rate, this is the watch—it looks like this. As to how I got my hands on it, on a wristwatch which is quite evidently as grand as this one is—yes, yes, it was from my father, it was my father's wristwatch—but it was my mother actually who actually gave it to me—or perhaps better to say, from whom I received it. You see, my father could not have passed this wristwatch along to me because my father was deceased at the time. Certain injuries in August. Of 1986, that is. To be sure, all of you out there, you will presently hear all there is to be said about how I came to cause these injuries. But getting back to the watch, I got it from my mother in 1988—whereas in respect of my father, I had done away with him as much maybe as two years previous. Well, dates, as I warned, as I said. All right, yes—it was definitely August of 1986. Anyway, it was by such means—I mean I disposed of my father by such means—that surely you must understand there cannot be any jeopardy to me in my making this declaration to you here this evening. No, no, you must not think that I would—that I, a husband, a father—would wittingly go out and court disaster. On the contrary, no harm can come to me from this—although I am a small man and am by nature routinely afraid enough to hear the rashness of such a declaration inflaming the fates, as they say. But done is done, as they also say. No going back to grab hold. Yes, yes, this light novel of ours is already under way. Anyway, the watch is an Audemars Piguet, I think it is pronounced. My eyes, even with my glasses on—and, as you must have by now observed, apart from my reading from my business card, there has been no other need for me up to now to put my glasses on tonight—my eyes are not good enough for me to tell you if it is a comma or if it is a hyphen that I see between the two words, the two names, or is it one name?—namely, between Audemars and Piguet—or whether it is just the teensiest of scratches that I am seeing when I study the space between them. In any case, yes, yes, there is definitely something there. Still, whatever it is that is there, even if it is an imperfection on the face of the watch of some kind, this Audemars Piguet of mine—or really of my father—that is, of Philip Lish—I suppose I should say—I expect I could probably get for it as much as twelve, say, to, say, fifteen thousand dollars for it. I mean, of this there can be no question—honestly. I mean, I honestly think you can give every credence to a figure somewhere between twelve probably and fifteen thousand dollars, my certainty being the result of the fact that the day after I got back up to New York from Florida with it—with my father's wristwatch, that is—I took myself over to the diamond district and went from shop to shop with it—you know, saying that I was giving every consideration to selling it, asking what I might get for it if I did, and receiving for my trouble maybe five or six offers, which offers—to adjust for the way these things work—doing business, I suppose you could call it—one enlarges by a certain factor, depending. Besides, this is 1990 and that was 1988—so doesn't one also have to allow for the steady pressure of inflation and so on? Look, I want you to appreciate the fact that when I say between twelve and fifteen thousand dollars, there is nothing capricious in such figures. But you are free to check for yourself—an Audemars Piguet—the watch will be right here with me when I step down from this stage—I will have no hesitation in letting you examine it and take down the particulars. For one thing, you will see what is incised onto the back of the case—you'll see 1962 on the back—because 1962, this was the date, this was the year, that this Audemars Piguet wristwatch of mine was given to my father by his brothers. Or probably I should say given to my father by my father's surviving brothers—because, of course, my father's brother Charley was long dead by the time of the gift, Charley having succumbed in 1944. Whereas this gift was conveyed to my father in 1962, so that it was Sam and Henry who were actually the ones who gave it to Dad—these were the Lish brothers who gave Dad this wristwatch. As a sort of going-away present, I think we might say. My dad's brothers—Sam and Henry—they were my father's partners in a company called Lish Brothers—and my father was leaving the company, he was going to go to Florida, my father was going to go away—so that, according to the story my father told me, this wristwatch was a sort of gesture his brothers were making, a statement of their—of Sam and Henry's—feeling for him, of their brotherly affection for him—because he was, Dad was, taking himself away from the prosecution of the family business, you see—he was going to pick up stakes and go down there to Florida, you see—and take his leave of Lish Brothers, which was the family business, you see—which, by the way, was an enterprise whose activity was the making of ladies' hats. Organized, as it happens, not long after the turn of the century—actually organized by that deceased brother I mentioned—actually organized by him, by Charles Lish, or Charley Lish—by Charley, the oldest of the brothers, and by Sam, who was the next-to-oldest brother, considering the four Lish brothers in all, among which four persons my father was the next-to-youngest, leaving Henry, of course, as that one, as the youngest one. So that what happened was that Charley and Sam were the brothers who first organized the firm—and then years later, really still as boys, Philip—did I tell you that my father's name was Philip? Yes, I did indeed, I think, tell you that my father's name was Philip—spelled P-H-I-L-I-P, by the way. Anyway, Charley and Sam finally took Philip and Henry into the business. When I do not know, I do not know what year—but so far as I was ever able to surmise, the year they took Dad in was some years after the firm of Lish Brothers had first been formed—which, by the way, was first in the business of dealing in feathers. Or at least this is my information—feathers for millinery. In due course, I suppose it was, Lish Brothers set itself to turning out all sorts of headwear for women—and became, in time, the largest manufacturer of the kind, or so it stated just under the line that said *Lish Brothers* on the company's official letterhead. But who said that this was a category of what I am up here for—how big or not big Lish Brothers was? What I was getting at was this—that my father's brothers talked my father into not taking his money out of the business even though he was going to take himself out of it. What my father got for this—not in exchange surely but probably as a sign of Sam and Henry's thanks to him for his doing it—was this wristwatch that you can see up here, this Audemars Piguet wristwatch that I was finally able to wrest away from my mother in December, or perhaps it was in January, of 1988—which wasn't, whenever it was, much before she died. Well, my father wanted to go live in Florida. My father wanted to pick up my mother and himself and go live in Florida—and not work any more but just to live out, as agreeably as he could, whatever was left of his life. In any case, my sister followed suit—took off from here in New York and took a place not too far from where Mother and Dad went. My sister Natalie, I suppose I should say—although, in fact, her name was really Lorraine. Except that my saying, she always claimed, "Rain, rain, go away, come again another day"—Natalie always claimed that I, Gordon, was always saying that, that when we were very young that I, Gordon, was always teasing her like that, and that that was why she had made our mother and father finally let her change her name to the name Natalie from the name Lorraine. But I cannot stand up here and truly say to you that I can remember my ever saying any such thing—"Rain, rain, go away, come again another day." All I can truly say is that I never did like the name Natalie and that, if it had been up to me, I would have stuck with the name Lorraine. I tell you, I am even willing to think that that was the finish for her, my sister, when she gave herself another name. In any event, she is dead. Natalie is dead. Dead with all the rest of the Lishes who went to die in Florida. Not that they all went down there to die, of course. No, no, only Charley went down there to do that. But Dad, for instance, he just went to Florida to have the best life he could get.

Until he died. Which, as I believe I have said, happened by my hand. This one—and this one. And these arms, this chest. Look at this wristwatch. Not possible for any of you to see it from where you are sitting, of course—but over here on the back of the case it says *For Phillip, Beloved Brother, 1962.* That's the inscription that my father's brothers Henry and Sam had caused to be engraved on this Audemars Piguet that the two of them got together to present my dad with when he went off to Florida. This is what it says—says, has said, from 1962, I ask you to realize, to this very day—to wit, *For Phillip, Beloved Brother.* And then there is the date. Philip spelled P-H-I-L-L-I-P. Philip is spelled Phillip—which report, as I have been saying, you are welcome to verify for yourself when I have finished with my struggle up here and am down among you again. Be certain of it—I am not only willing to show the watch to you, I am actually hoping and praying to show the watch to you. Indeed, it would please me very greatly to have you inspect the watch and perhaps even to conceive a certain enthusiasm for this watch. Look, I won't shilly-shally with you about it—quite frankly, it has been in my mind to see if I can make a deal for this watch. Very frankly, it is beginning to look to me as if I could really start to do with the money right now. No question about it, it would really be wonderful for me and mine if I could start to get together a goodish supply of extra cash right now. Because, let's face it, I, we—we are going to need it. If you take the conditions that aroused me to stand up here and speak to you like this in the first place, then, yes, I am positively going to need as much as I can get of it, I think. Of money, I mean. Because these exorbitant circumstances that I have been hinting at, there is no question about it, they are going to call on every resource I've got going, money not excluded—so, please, please, if you feel yourself at all inspired to inquire further into this watch, then please do feel yourself invited to propose yourself as the next one to have it. By all means, yes, yes, there is absolutely no impediment, not certainly any from my point of view, why any one of you might not go out of here tonight in possession of this device that you see up here, whose inscription, when I finally saw it, the engraving, in 1988—by the way, saw it, I should say, as the result of, I should say, of an episode wherein I had been required to help her—to help my mother, that is—make her way to the toilet from her bed. Mind you, she had not, my mother had not—at the time, you understand—stood upon her feet for a period of, well, we can guess accurately enough, I think—not once, according to the companion my mother then had for herself, a nurse, this nurse, a sort of practical nurse, for about a period of, I would say, or the nurse said, about a year and a half. To the toilet from the bed—my mother required me to help her make her way, you understand, to the toilet from her bed. Well, I can tell you, my mother was quite naked at the time. And was, since she was five years my father's senior—please know that my mother was five years my father's senior—my mother was ninety-three years of age at the time—well, my point is that the woman was, in her nakedness, so very frail-looking. Frail-looking or fragile-looking or, yes, yes, actually very breakable-looking, you see—such a petite woman, a woman of so many years, a leaf, a dry leaf—and absolutely naked too, you see—who had not been out of her bed for as much as—that's it—about a year and a half. But the thing that was happening, you see—what my mother was all of a sudden out of the blue, what she had suddenly decided she wanted was for me to help her make her way from her bed—oh, yes, it goes without saying that we were going to have to make our way, of course, around past the foot of my father's old bed—into the toilet, if you can believe it—and for me to then actually have to then sit with her there. But really, I do not think that you could possibly understand what I mean by sit with my mother there. I mean, my mother wanted for me to sit with her there. Well, as you know, as I said, the woman did always, of course, have a companion with her, of course. After all, my mother had quite a lot of money at her disposal—and could well afford the attentions of a sort of practical nurse. Or actually three separate shifts of them. No, no, she was a spender—my mother was a spender. Unlike my father—my God, my mother was nothing like my father in these respects. Not in the least, my mother was not in the least an exceptional person in these respects—in the sense that there was no one in our family who was more saving, I suppose you could say—thriftier, then, more careful with a dollar, say—than my father was. Unless, of course, it would be, of course, myself. I do not think anyone could be more prudent than I am. And with every red cent, you can depend upon it. Anyway, yes, of course, my mother had nothing to deter her from her always having a practical nurse with her on hand—three shifts of them, three such attendants in constant attendance upon her, attention around-the-clock, you would say. But she wanted me.

My mother wanted me. Would have no other but me. To take her to the toilet, I mean. Wanted suddenly to get up like that after a year, they said at least it was, on her back. And thereafter for me to sit with her there. My mother wanted for me to be the one who would hold her when she got there. Because my mother wanted to be held—really had to be held—and wanted me to be the one who would hold on to her on the toilet so that she would not be in any danger of falling off the toilet. No, no, this is not guesswork—this is what my mother said. So, you see, it was not until I had done exactly what my mother had wanted for me to do that she finally gave me this wristwatch, which I already had, in a manner of speaking, committed a sort of crime for. At all events, I had always expected that, once I had this wristwatch on my wrist, that when my father's wristwatch eventually came into my keeping, that it would prove to be too tight for me. For my wrist, I mean. Because from looking at the wristwatch on my father's wrist, I just took it for granted that the watch would make for a tighter fit when it finally got on my wrist. But, as you will see for yourself if you are one of the ones who I hope and pray will ask to have a look at it on me tonight, or off me, it's—the watch is—contrary to all expectation, rather remarkably too loose for this wrist of mine. Big for my wrist—actually really for either of my wrists—by a not insignificant number of links. These tiny little links. Whereas, as I must have said, my father is a small man—or anyhow was a small man. Well, to be sure, I am a small man, I am not saying that I am not a small man. But my father—I tell you, you can depend on this—he was noticeably, I always thought at least, the smaller man. Between us, I mean. At least, anyway, the shorter one. Which brings us to the Crosley. Because insofar as the Crosley is concerned, I can actually furnish a sort of proof, I suppose you could say, of how small, or anyhow of how short at least, my father was. If I can advert to the time when I saw the Crosley, which, by the bye, was, I think, 1944. Namely, in the little tiny living room of the little tiny house that Lish Brothers—not the men but the business, I mean—the company rather than the persons who owned it—well, Dad told me that it was Lish Brothers that was paying for it—had rented the little tiny house for Charley Lish to die in. In Florida. Well, I am sure that I must have mentioned the fact that Charley was the first of the brothers to die—and, as I believe I must also have said, it was in Florida that Charley died. But did I say of cancer?

Of the intestines, I think I heard someone say. Or of the bowel. Because I believe that it was on the Orange Blossom Special—going down or coming back up—that I heard someone say that it was the intestines. Or bowel—I think I maybe heard bowel. You know, Charley, Sam, Henry, they all died of cancer. Philip is the only one of them who didn't. I had not really ever thought of this before—namely, that Dad was the only one who did not die of cancer. Well, he didn't. But as to the proof I was promising, if you will please forgive the word, because of course I realize that what I am going to put before you proves, I realize, positively nothing—but the fact is that there was a nurse in the room—in Uncle Charley's little tiny living room. There was a nurse sitting with us—or with Uncle Charley, I should say—because the nurse was sitting with Uncle Charley on the little two-seater affair, sitting next to Charley on it—whereas the rest of us—Dad and my uncle Henry and my uncle Sam and their sons, we were all sitting across from the two-seater on just wooden chairs. Did I tell you that it was just the sons who went down to Florida with the fathers? Because, so far as I know, none of my other cousins went down, the girls. Not that I know the reason for it. I never even inquired into the reason for it. Was it a custom to do with our religion, do you think? Or with just my family's way of doing things in the matter of paying your last respects? Whatever it was, it was only the sons among us who went along with the fathers when the fathers went down to Florida to pay their last respects to their brother Charley. Natalie—was she still Lorraine then?—I can certainly vouch for the fact that Natalie was not there with us then. Anyway, so far as I can remember, every day that we went there to see Uncle Charley in that little tiny living room, it had just the fathers and the sons sitting in it—and not one of them, not one of the fathers, was as tall as the woman was. As the nurse was—who was sitting on a kind of two-seater affair with Uncle Charley sitting next to her. Who himself sat there—or so I saw the days that my father and I went there from the hotel where we were all staying—it was either the Sea Isle or it was the Versailles—and where I, whichever one it was, was getting my regular daily sunbaths up on the roof where, whichever hotel it was, it had a solarium—who himself was sitting there in his pajamas. It seemed nice to me, it seemed very familylike to me, the fact that Charley was never not—when I went there with my father to the little house—not sitting in pajamas. But coming back to the question of what made me think of the Crosley, no, anyone could see that there was nobody in the room who was as tall as the nurse was even with everybody sitting down. Take Charley, for instance, who was sitting right next to her up on an air cushion, if this is what you call those contrivances. Namely, the ones meant to keep toddlers and the like safe in the water. Because Uncle Charley was sitting up on one of them. But the point is that, even though he was, and that even though it probably made him two, maybe three, inches taller than he was, the air cushion still did not make Uncle Charley even as tall as the nurse. Sitting, of course. Because this is how I was seeing this, with them both sitting, of course. Not that the nurse was not also taller, I could also see, than also Sam and Henry and Dad. She was easily—even seated, even with all of them seated, anyone could tell—taller than any of them were. But further to the point, even with Charley's extra inches, even with the additional inches added to him by his station up on the air cushion, Charley was still short next to the nurse, judging from the comparison you could easily make between them when they were both sitting next to one another on the two-seater affair. But, of course, when we all sat there, I never saw Uncle Charley anything but seated. The days Dad and I went from—yes, it was the Versailles and not the Sea Isle that we went from, it must have been the Versailles which was the hotel where I went up onto the roof to the solarium every morning and every afternoon except for the middle of the day when we all got in some taxicabs and went to see Uncle Charley—anyway, the days that Dad took me with him there to the little rented house for us all to sit in Uncle Charley's little living room with him, Uncle Charley was always in the same place, always there on the little two-seater, always sitting up there on it on the air cushion. But the nurse sometimes got up. In relation to the Crosley, that is. Because, you see, there was a little tiny refrigerator, a sort of pint-sized refrigerator, a little Crosley refrigerator, there with us in the little living room. Which is to say that it was right there in the middle of the room with us, right there with us between the two-seater affair that Charley and the nurse were sitting on, between the two-seater affair, on the one hand, and the row, in effect, of wooden chairs that the rest of us were sitting on—Dad and myself and my uncles and my cousins, that is. Well, how could I not notice that this little refrigerator was a Crosley? I mean, first imagine the circumstances—death and so forth. And there it was, sitting right there with us there in the living room and not, as one would expect, in the kitchen. Bear in mind, please, that I was ten years old at the time and that I had therefore seen my fair share of refrigerators. After all, you go home to somebody's house after school for milk and cookies and a look at the house, it never fails but that you make yourself aware of that household's make of refrigerator. Granted, this might have been a peculiar form of attention for a boy, a concern of any kind with the makes of things. But I can positively attest to sitting in the kitchens of other people's houses and making it a point of making myself aware of which company made the refrigerator. You know, Westinghouse, Kelvinator, Norge, Coldpoint, Amana, Admiral, Frigidaire, General Electric—these were the makes of refrigerator I think I probably knew about. Something like the Sea Isle or the Versailles, something like this I admit to my not being entirely positive about. But I really knew my refrigerators. By the time I was ten years old, I mean. And a Crosley, a refrigerator called a Crosley, this was certainly a novelty to me, I can tell you. Which made it queerly exhilarating, I think—a new make of refrigerator, a tiny little refrigerator, a Crosley. Plus the fact that it was situated as it was—namely, there with us in the living room as a sort of centerpiece between us. Or is it among us? Well, I admit it, it was all of it very exciting to me—queerly exhilarating, I think I said. Which effect, I must tell you—I didn't tell you yet, did I?—which effect was enhanced, if this is the word, by the fact that the Crosley was always dripping. It was constantly, constantly dripping. I mean, imagine it—my uncle never speaking, Charley never speaking, Charley just sitting up there sleeping on the air cushion like that, or sort of up on it half-sleeping like that—and meanwhile the little Crosley always so constantly dripping like that. It was incessant, I tell you. Arranged, as it was, there in the little living room like that—and never not ceaselessly dripping. And not to forget the woman sitting with us, the nurse—so tall, she was so tall. Unless I was just seeing for the first time how small all of the Lishes were. But what I did not tell you yet, what I have not told you yet, is that from time to time, she, the nurse, she gets to her feet and goes on over to the little Crosley. Which was a distance of what? Of no more than a stride or two for her at the most, at the absolute most. In any event, the woman gets up from where she is sitting and takes the step or two it takes for her to position herself in front of the Crosley. Well, it took her nothing to get there, you understand, so small was this sitting space, this little tiny living room. I mean, it was something for me to reckon with, the fact that these Lish brothers would contrive to rent for their brother—who was dying, mind you, dying—such a little tiny house of the perfectly dismissive size that that one was of. I tell you, this living room, it was like a toy living room. But I suppose one really has to sharpen one's notion of how extraordinarily frugal these men were—that as well-heeled as they were, that they were nevertheless so ferocious in their close stewardship of every nickel they ever had in their hands. No, no, please to see this as I see this—these were not grasping men, my father and his brothers, no, no, no. My father and his brothers, it would be entirely wide of the mark for me to suggest to you that these were grasping men. But, yes, once the money was in their hands—ah, yes, this, I think, was a very different matter for them, indeed, holding on to what they had. For as the evidence asserts—well, I ask you, doesn't that tiny little house speak for itself? No, no, if it was money they had in their hands, then it was not easy for these men to let it be money that got out of their hands. Or so it seemed to me. Mind you, however,

I stand here and point the finger at no one. For make no mistake of it, my own husbanding of a dollar is probably more uxorious than could ever have been said for any of them—for Sam or Henry, or for Dad or Charley. But one is a dope to enforce a comparison between such things. Nonsense to suggest that anyone can make a measurement between such things. Or even between any things. It is just that I do not want for you to anticipate that you might be coming up against some sort of a pushover, should you have it in mind to make me an offer on this Audemars Piguet of mine tonight. Be alert—I am an expert on the value of this thing and intend to insist on every iota of it when the time comes for me to take my leave of you tonight. Yes, I may have killed him, yes, but I want you to know that I am my father's son—and let there be no mistake of this, please. Believe me, you do not see me buying Squibb when I can walk an extra block or two—or twenty!—and buy Rite-Aid. I mean, respecting this regimen I was talking about, the protocol involving methoxsalen—which, you may have forgotten, is the substance I take in order to potentiate the value to me of what is present to me in ultraviolet light. Concerning my psoriasis, that is. I mean, as I must have already made mention of, all my life—or at least since the seventh year of my life—I have been a seeker of light. Or really, I should say, not of light but of ultraviolet light. Because of my psoriasis, you understand. Positively not, never ever Squibb's, you may be sure of it—you would never catch me laying out good money for a bottle of Squibb's when, God knows, there is even the least prospect that, with a certain reasonable effort, I might find myself a less costly brand. Of mineral oil, I mean. As to the Rite-Aid brand, this is the label I have been buying in recent years, given that Rite-Aid runs you roughly sixty-four cents less than it is going to cost you for every other discounted brand I have ever been able to catch sight of in my neighborhood or, for that matter, down in the one where the Random House building is—this, mind you, for the thirty-two-ounce bottle. Even Swan, or even White Cross, or even Lubinol—none of them has a price on their thirty-two-ounce bottle that appeals to me with the convincing argument that, I can tell you, the Rite-Aid label does. No, no, I am a Rite-Aid customer for all of my mineral oil supplies, and make no mistake of it! My God, the years of mineral oil, it must be by now gallons and gallons of it. What are the words? Slather, lather? Lord, yes, I fairly coat myself with the stuff. Which is because I positively have to. Because you have to bear in mind how punishing it can be to your skin—the sunlight, I mean, the sunlight!—if you do not mediate it to whatever certain extent by reason of a good protective coating. Of mineral oil, I mean. Lord, you cannot possibly realize! Take sixty milligrams of methoxsalen, take four capsules of methoxsalen, and not make certain that you have a generous layer of mineral oil on you all over you—heaven help you, I don't care how tough your skin is, I am here to tell you that you are going out of your way to ask for trouble when you make your way out-of-doors to go sit in even the haziest light. Or even in just the kind of grisly glow you get in New York when, from rim to rim, the sky is dead. Be certain of it, this methoxsalen that I am made to take in order for my skin to extract from the light the good work that the light can do—even when it is not the sort of light that one would actually regard as sunlight—it packs a wallop, be certain of it. Whereas there is nothing for me to be particularly fretful about if I have taken the appropriate precautions. Namely, of chief importance, applied mineral oil, applied to myself a good heavy grade of mineral oil. Oh, but not that the wearing of goggles is really of any less importance. You see, don't you? I mean, can you not see how so much of my life has had to be dedicated to such concerns? But perhaps you did not quite take my meaning yet. I mean, it's this psoriasis that I have always had—or have anyway had since I was seven, that is. Because it's made it so that sun—sunshine, the sunlight—this has been what so much of my life has been—always chasing the light. Which was why the discovery of methoxsalen was such a bonanza for me, given that I did not have to have the sun in the sense that you would interpret this to mean. Oh, to be sure, the sunshine in Florida, this was still wonderful for me, to be sure—as would obviously be the case for the Arizona sun, for the immense sunshine that I once went out to Arizona for. Which tells you what it was that once got me out there, as I said at the outset, playing cowboy. Oh, don't think I did not like the posing and the pretending and the making-believe, all right. But it was the sunshine that was actually at the bottom of it. I tell you, I can stand up here tonight and still feel the furnace of it. Nothing make-believe about Gila Bend. It was such a great thing for me, the sun in the desert. You must have heard of Gila Bend. But notice, with the advent in my life of methotrexate, on the one hand, and of methoxsalen, on the other, it was possible for me to come back and live back home here back in New York, provided, of course, that I be conscientious in keeping to the regular sunbathing procedure that I am required to observe. Oh, but it is really an ancient labor with me, these exertions of mine to keep getting my skin into the light. And for my mother and father—oh, what a job it must have been for them. I mean, quite obviously, my parents must have paid an awful price to do what they could to arrange it so that I could always be within reach of the light. Which doubtless explains why it was that I was not left home—as Natalie was, even though, of course, Natalie was older than I was—when it came to the matter of whether or not I should be included among the cousins who were going to be going down there to Florida to say goodbye to Uncle Charley. Inasmuch as, you have to appreciate this, I was the youngest. Of all the cousins, I was the youngest. So that it probably was not all that necessary that I be there among those who were going to be present when the fathers and the sons went to pay their last respects. Especially considering the money. Especially, too, considering that this was 1944 and that there was a war going on at the time and that, to get the tickets for the train, it was going to mean paying off some people under the table, my father said. I only mean to say that for my dad to take me along with him quite obviously must have represented a sort of hardship for him—or, let us say, no little difficulty at least. Because over and above what it was going to cost for the tickets, over and above the official fare for me to go down with him on the train, for me to go along with Dad, it was quite definitely going to cost him a not dismissable outlay of cash—or so Dad said. Which offers us an index—does it not?—of how terrible the lesions must have got by the time I was ten and, too, of how greatly Dad must have wanted to do what he could for me, for me to achieve some relief from them. Because the itching, I can tell you, it was furious. I was always in a kind of a fury with it. With the itching and the bleeding and the scaling—always fissures opening up. Jesus, talk about what I can right this instant feel standing up here like this. Just the itching, there was no end to it. Even when you had torn all the skin off, it was still down there somewhere, so that you just kept clawing at yourself until you were sort of all ripped open but still itching. So, I mean, quite obviously—my father must have been in search of whatever could be done for me, whatever relief could be had. And at whatever expense, I mean. I mean, the picture I have of it, it is of my father so frantic. Because, you know, it must have been no simple matter just to pick yourself up and undertake to travel somewhere by train in those days, given that the trains—as not very many of you, given your age, would have any way of knowing, I suppose—the trains, the railroads, they were largely given over in those days to conducting their affairs, I understand, in accordance with everybody getting together with the national effort. So that for mere civilians to just step on board and go somewhere—well, as my father on this point was quite specific with me, some cash had to be passed around to certain persons. It was winter. I was taken out of school. It was, I think, February, in fact. I mean to say that it was so exciting for me—Florida, my God!—you cannot imagine it. It was my first time. Just the fact that there was suddenly, when we got to Jacksonville, I think it was, no snow. And then that it started getting even warm—and then even hot. My God. Delray Beach, for example, and so on. So you can see the specialness of it for me, that it was heaven-sent, as the saying goes—on the one hand, the necessity of the family errand, whereas, on the other, the lovely benison of the sun. But that was not a felicitious choice—errand. I should not have said errand. Because for my father, of course, as my father on the Orange Blossom Special, I must tell you, again and again kept making very clear to everybody—his relations with his brother Charley, they were unusually strong as far as my father was concerned, they were unusually meaningful as far as my father was concerned, as he kept over and over again telling everybody, no offense to any of them intended. None intended to Sam or Henry, I mean. Or mean that Dad said he meant none. Namely, when Dad kept telling this story he was telling us all. On the way down. Or it could have been that it was on the way back up. But it was when we were all on the Orange Blossom Special, all right—of this I am absolutely, I can assure you, sure. Namely, that my father kept saying to everybody that he felt that he had a right to be closer to his brother Charley than any of us did, given the fact that there had been the famous time when Dad was probably going to choke to death, actually be asphyxiated, except that he had popped up out of the blue and taken charge in the nick of time—Charley. Charley had. By the bye, have I told you yet that the Venetian blinds there in the little living room that we were all sitting in, have I managed to tell you yet how the blinds were always kept somewhat closed? So, you see, the light in there in that little tiny room was always dusky, you might say. Muted. In any event, I kept sitting there thinking such restless thoughts. To tell you the truth, it made me very uneasy, sitting there in that little room like that with the light so muted, and therefore so useless to me—when outside, if they would just let me get back out there outside, I knew that the light was supposed to be doing so much good for me. Or so I remember Dad constantly telling me. And yet there I was, having to sit there for about as much as an hour or more right there in the middle of the best part of the day. And day after precious day! In a dark room. Or, all right, in a darkened room. It was really, I think I have to tell you, a very strange thing for me. Sitting there like that—for however many days it actually was—because I cannot really remember how many days of sitting with Uncle Charley like that it actually was. How many times we had to all go down and get in taxicabs and go over to see him instead of all of us staying in the sun at the Versailles. Because that was definitely it, a place called the Versailles and not the Sea Isle. At any rate, I think it must have been a very trying experience for me. Not to mention my having to hear the Crosley constantly dripping and dripping like that—with her, with the nurse every so often getting herself to her feet and taking that one step or so that was all she needed to get herself to the Crosley, then reaching her hand down there underneath it to feel around in there underneath it for the drip tray, which she would then slide out and very, very gingerly lift, getting it up in her hands very, very carefully, whereupon I would see her go with it to the door, take another two steps to the door, open it, open the door, and then fling the contents of it—whatever was there in the drip tray, that is—out there out onto the little oblong of funny-looking awful grass that they had out there. And I would see—have I told you this yet?—I would see such a flash of light. Oh, no, but this was not the only thing which the nurse kept making it her business to do when we all would be sitting there with her when we were sitting with my father's brother Charley—because just as often as the nurse went and got the drip tray out to get rid of whatever it was that had dripped down into it, she also got up to take herself a look inside of it. Inside of the Crosley, I mean. I mean, that the nurse would just go over to the Crosley and then squat down in front of it and then pull open the little door and then take a look there inside of the little refrigerator and then close it all back up again. Her having done nothing but look, I mean. In any case, the point that I was trying to make is that getting out out-of-doors and getting all of the sunlight I could, this was the principal theme of my childhood—and actually, for that matter, has been no less of a one in my manhood, I suppose you could say. These clothes that I wear, for example, these clothes that you see me wearing, they are the clothes that I always wear. I mean, this particular costume—this shirt, these trousers—I have a closet that has nothing in it but more of these very same items. I swear it to you—more washable trousers just like these, probably as many as ten more washable shirts just like this one that you see. There are persons among you who know me, who have, over the years, seen me from time to time, and they could tell you, yes, that this is how I dress, that this is how I always dress—these very things almost always. The only difference is that tonight you see me with a sport coat on, with a necktie on. But these trousers—if I step away from the lectern, you see these trousers?—these are the kind of trousers I always wear, washable—and this shirt—these tan items, these, they call them, suntan-colored items. I mean, I have never before made this statement before—but this is why I wear these particular clothes, not just because I save so much money on dry cleaning but also because of this color, this particular kind of suntan color. And everything on me so loose. With all of my things always fitting me so loose. Everything I wear—so big. Because these things that you see are much bigger than I need for them to be. Everything I buy, I always buy it a size or three bigger than I really need for it to be. But, no, no, it is not for style. I do not do what I do for style. It may appear to be a style—but, no, style does not have anything to do with it really. It is really a sort of necessity for me. At all events, you will always see me favoring clothes that have this particular sort of colorless color to them and that are far too big for me when it comes to fit. But for necessity, for necessity's sake, please believe me. Namely, the oil, you see—namely, it is because of the oil, you see. Because after I have had one of my sunbathing sessions, after I have taken the methoxsalen and been up on the roof and had one of my noontime workday methoxsalen sunbathing sessions, there is then the vexatious matter of getting myself back to my office looking at least approximately presentable. Because, as you may remember from Bill Roberson's introductory notes on me, I work in an office, you see—and these colors, this suntan color, it helps to camouflage the blots of mineral oil that are impossible for me to keep from getting on me. I can rub and rub with the towel that I am always taking with me with my manuscripts up onto the roof with me, yet no matter how much I rub, there is bound to always be some residue. After I have clocked my time up there, after I have had an exposure that was sufficiently long for me, given the power of the sixty milligrams, then I have to wipe myself off and get back into my clothes. But is it ever possible to get all of it off? The mineral oil, I mean. No, no, it never fails but that there is always going to be some ghost of oil on me somewhere. Which is why these clothes—bought loose-fitting in order for me to forfend against there being overmuch contact between them and the skin. Well, to be sure, there will always be blotting—there is nothing that can ever be thoroughly done about the blotting. But it stands to reason that the looser my clothes are, the less oil that is going to be blotted up. Thus, my practice of always wearing such loose-fitting clothes—whereas respecting the color of them, experience has taught me—and taught Barbara, I might add—that it is the color that best disguises the stains that will eventually—ineluctably—collect around all over me. All over whatever I wear. Oh, Barbara, when she was able, when

Barbara still had the strength to be able, she used to use every manner of aggressive detergent on them, all sorts of pre-wash recipes—even, as I remember it, a pretty successful paste made up from mashing Clorox granules into a mixture of Top Job and Lestoil. But the results are—were, really—never more than partial. Or only fractionally effective, I suppose I should say. So that I have, if you care to look, these faintly darkened patches on absolutely everything I ever wear—dots, spots, all blots—sometimes big blotches that sometimes seem to me to be shadows of the lesions underneath. At any rate, you will be able to see all of this for yourself, if you wish, if you prove to be one of the ones who elect to take a close look at this vintage 1962 Audemars Piguet that I have up here—and who thereafter might be persuaded to quote me an offer on it. Well, you already saw for yourself how oversized these trouser pockets of mine are, given the trial it was for me to fish this little business card of mine I made my notes on out of them. A tenth of whiskey hardly speaks to it. Because the fact is that I can put a whole bottle of mineral oil in one of these pockets. I can actually fit a thirty-two-ounce-size bottle of Rite-Aid mineral oil in one of these pockets of mine and then go ahead and walk around my office with it with nobody, as far as I know, any the wiser. Or, time was—before I could not do it any more because of the methotrexate and what it does to your liver—time was when I would walk around with not a tenth but with a serious bottle in one of these pockets. Of brandy, I suppose I should say, given that Metaxa is brandy officially. I suppose that Metaxa is officially brandy. Oh, I admit it, there is no denying it, that I can stand up here and smell it, breathe it—feel it scorching its way down into me. But I have to say that I am glad that neither Salter nor Bell, nor any of the others whom I annoyed when I went around whispering for it out in the lobby out there—I have to say that I am glad that none of you proved forthcoming with anything for me. Not that I mind saying I miss it. If ever in my life I have missed it, tonight I really miss it. But, mind you, I want you to know that it was never the whiskey that got in the way of my work—that if it was anything that ever got in the way of my work, it was the troubling task of my having to manage to get clearance during the course of the workday—this, you will understand, so that the methoxsalen might get a chance to work its miracle on me. So that this, then, was an unbudgeable condition in whatever terms I came to with a prospective employer.

Unbudgeable, unbudgeable. Take the case with *Esquire,* for example. Because, as you heard Bill Roberson say, there was a time—for eight years I believe it was—when I was attached to *Esquire* magazine. When I did the fiction for the magazine. Eight years, I think it was, or maybe it was only seven. In any event, why I was even there in the first place, it had no little to do with the exceptional arrangement that my employers were willing to make for me there. Namely, Gingrich and Hayes. Namely, Arnold Gingrich and Harold Hayes. Both deceased now, it grieves me to say. Yes, yes, cancer again, in both cases cancer again—the lungs in the case of Gingrich, the brain in the case of Hayes. And, oh yes, throat, it was a cancer of the throat in the case of still another of my seniors at *Esquire* who had gone ahead and intervened on my behalf. Erickson, I mean—a fellow named Don Erickson, I mean. All dead, all three of them, cancers, all three. But where was I? Hey, I just felt a certain dizziness—the card, the card—just for an instant. Yes, Hayes. Hayes, Gingrich, Don Erickson, they were all three of them in on it, had all three connived with someone crucial in the building—which was, by the way, not the building where the magazine's offices, in its most recent permutation, are located. That being, that building that I was once in, being the one at 488 Madison Avenue. Namely, between Fifty-second Street and Fifty-first. So you can see that I didn't really have to go all over the city when I got fired from *Esquire* and had to go over to the Random House building for Knopf, for the job that I now have at Knopf—the Knopf address, the Random House address, being at the corner of Third Avenue and Fiftieth Street. Anyway, that was the address where *Esquire* then was—namely, if you are talking about the years from 1969 to 1976—which, yes, now that I hear myself say this, I realize that makes it not eight years that I was there but seven. Because I was fired from *Esquire* in 1976. But, no, no, just for the record, not fired from *Esquire* by any of the persons whose names I just named. Fired from *Esquire* by a whole different crew of people, by completely different kinds of fellows indeed. But getting back to my point, Hayes and Gingrich and Erickson, they had worked it all out for me, they had all got together and worked it all out for me. How they were able to do it I don't know—it may have been via some custodian or something. I mean, I am certain it was probably all completely unofficial. But the gist of it is that clearance, if this is the word, was gained. I mean, it was permissable for me to make my way up to the roof. Did it mean that there were certain persons who had to look the other way? Look, I cannot tell you what the details of it were. All I can say is that I would go get on an elevator, go up to the topmost floor, then go the rest of the way by stairway—and then, with my own key, you understand—because naturally it was a fire law, that door, that last door, the janitors had to always check it to make sure it was locked—with my own key I would unlock that door and go right out. Imagine it, an office building in New York, in midtown New York, imagine your being up on the roof of it. Because for all those years I was. Lunchtimes. The lunch hour, so called. This was always when I did this—always during when I was free to go out for lunch. It felt like—it felt like access to me. Access had been acquired for me. My psoriasis, you see, it was a kind of license. Oh, I can't tell you, I cannot possibly tell you what it was like for me—swallowing the four capsules, the methoxsalen, I mean. I had a big tote bag of Barbara's with me. I had a big tote bag of Barbara's that I started taking with me to the office with me—and I would put some manuscripts in it. I would go to the water fountain and take the methoxsalen and then go back to my office and get enough manuscripts for me to work on—and then I would put everything down into the big tote bag of Barbara's that I still have a habit of using—put manuscripts in it, a towel in it, plus plenty of felt-tips and my mineral oil, of course, the Rite-Aid. Also, first and foremost, my goggles, of course. My God, of course, my goggles. God help you if you ever went up there without having your goggles with you. In the nude, you understand—I would go out there and sit out there very nearly in the nude, you understand. Which is a still further reason why I have the practice of always favoring these oversized chino trousers you see me wearing. Namely, because, as you can also see—here, wait a minute—I am going to have to step away from the lectern for a little bit and therefore be out of range of the microphone for a little bit. Here—do you see these shoes? Because, you see, I always wear these big shoes. Sort of like lace-up boots—or hightop shoes. Which accounts for still a further virtue of these loose-fitting pants I wear, given that it is no great maneuver for me to squat down up there on some roof and scoot these big baggy-legged trousers of mine down off over these big hightop shoes of mine without my having to take the shoes off. Because it happens that these are the shoes I wear. Indeed, they are the only manner of shoe I wear—high-topped and thick-soled and big-heeled. And, as must be evident from even a distance, they're pretty bulky, you understand. Actually, I get them from the Lotus people. For years and years now—really since ever since I came back from Gila Bend to New York—I have been wearing this very shoe, ordering it by mail from the Lotus people—who are the only ones, I think, who make it. Quite frankly, what animates me to go to so much bother for them is the impression that I have that a pair of these adds to the look of bulk I like to have in my appearance. Or, if not that, then certainly there is a decisive addition to how tall I stand. Or, let us just say, to how short I don't stand. Which is really a rather fatiguing distraction for me when I am in the company of anyone tall. Whereas it is almost, you might say, hopelessly disabling for me to have to be in the presense of anyone so assertively tall as is, say, Denis Donoghue, say. Even, for that matter, even with my father, even when I just had to stand somewhere with my father, for that matter, it mattered to me to feel that I had a little extra height to me. In any event, make no mistake of it, I had these very shoes on. This very pair. At the time, I mean. When it happened, I mean. Well, the fact is that I never, when I am out somewhere where people can get a look at me, where they might come up and get a good look at me, I never risk letting myself be discovered without my having them on—my shoes, I mean. In other words, even though I might be sitting somewhere almost nude, as it were, I still will be sitting there with my shoes on. Which is what they were at the Harbor House Apartments when what happened killed my father. As a matter of fact, I had taken them into account actually. Actually, I had made it my business to sit there and make sure that I was taking them into account actually. These shoes, I mean—their big heels, their thick soles. Whatever it came to, the additional elevation. Indeed, I can tell you that it was just the day previous to my going down there that I had gone ahead and had them reheeled. Because I can assure you that it is no ordeal for me at all for me to recall a detail of this kind—namely, the fact that it occurred to me that I had just had these shoes of mine reheeled. I mean—when I say occurred, what I mean is while I was on the telephone talking to Mother. In other words, Mother—or maybe it was Natalie, I don't remember—Mother, let us go ahead and say, was saying that I had to hurry up and come down there, and so it just popped into my head that thank God that I had just had this particular pair of these shoes of mine reheeled. Well, I always have at least two pair of them on hand. And this pair, the pair that I am wearing tonight—these were, and still are, my better pair, my less distressed pair, the pair I would naturally take with me if I were to go on a trip anywhere—and I was just marveling to myself about how what a piece of good luck it was that I had just happened to have had them, as recently as the day previous, reheeled. Previous, that is, to the day that Mother called. Or it may have been Natalie who did. Because I can distinctly remember my thinking about this—thinking that if I did go, then I really was ready to go. Plus taps. Plus, of course, brand-new taps. Because this is another habitual thing with me—namely, wearing taps on my heels. Preserves the life of the heel, you see. Therefore conserves the little extra lift it gives you. Well, please, I am not at all unaware of the fact that it must seem to you not a little ridiculous that a man would sit in his shorts like that up on a roof like that with any shoes on, let alone with ones like these. But I am asking for you to make allowances for the anxiety that I have been trying to find a way to describe to you. Up on the roof it sometimes really gets almost out of control for me. Out in the open like that.

My clothes nearly all off. The lesions. No, no, I really feel that I cannot risk my being surprised by someone when that is how I am—out there like that, not covered up by anything, the lesions. After all, if anyone came up, he would see me. Which is the sense in which the shoes help. I mean, in the sense that I feel that they are comforting. Because it would just exaggerate matters for me—aggravate them for me, I mean. Namely, if someone came up and I had to suddenly stand up—get to my feet and be barefooted. No, no, it would be awful enough just having my lesions seen. But perhaps you do not understand yet—the fact that there are blotches all over me. No, no, it is all absolutely unacceptable to me—I can tell you. Even the idea of it makes me afraid. Which is why, I repeat, these loose-fitting trousers. In other words, the fact that they work out just right for me—namely, in that I can get them off and then get them back on again without the shoes representing any sort of notable interference to my doing it. Not that anybody ever came up and caught me up on the roof at *Esquire*. No, no—no one ever came up and caught me asleep at the switch up there, I can tell you. Nor, please be sure, would I have been—in August of 1986—out there sunning myself alongside the pool at the Harbor

House Apartments if there had been anyone out there who could see me. Apart from my father, of course. Oh, yes, the attendant—well, yes, apart from my father and also the pool attendant, of course. But no, no, heat like that, there was no chance of there being anyone else out there. Because I really cannot stand it for people to see me with my lesions. But no, the pool attendant at the Harbor House Apartments, he really sort of kept himself concealed. Or have I not told you? Namely, that all this happened in Bal Harbour, Florida—specifically at the Harbor House Apartments. For this, as you must have surmised, was where my father and mother had moved from New York to—in 1962. To Bal Harbour. In other words, this was where I did this thing that I did which had the result of killing my father. To narrow it down even more for you, it was not in his apartment but was out at the pool. I mean, there over at the deep-end side of the cement apron that they have that runs all around the perimeter of the swimming pool. Which was where we were sitting, there on the apron alongside where there was the deep end of the pool. Which is to say, when I went down to sit with Dad because of Mother's call. If it was really Mother's and not Natalie's. In any event, in August of 1986, as I think I must have several times said by now. He had asked—not he, no, not my father—it was my mother or it was Natalie who had asked—for me to visit with him down there. Much in the manner, I myself could not help but think, the Lishes and their sons had once gone down to sit with Charley. But this was not cancer. It was the esophagus. Not that you cannot get a cancer in your esophagus. There is nothing to stop you from getting a cancer in your esophagus. But my father had no cancer in his esophagus. No, no, it was a stricture—he had a stricture. Dad had some kind of a stricture there, they said. His foodpipe, Dad's foodpipe—it had developed, they said, some sort of spontaneous erratic pattern of sudden constrictions in it. Suddenly, for no reason anybody was certain of, a certain section of the conduit would suddenly seize up on Dad, squeeze shut on him—or at least collapse enough to close everything off. Anything could do it. It did not even take his own saliva to do it. Just breathing could probably do it. Suddenly, for no apparent reason, Dad could suddenly cough, gag, choke. Or so Mother said. Unless it was Natalie who did. But I do not think that it could have been Natalie. I do not think that there could have been any discussion of this between Natalie and me. Absence had changed nothing between us. As brother and sister, we had always been at each other's throat. The fact that Natalie had gone off to Florida and inserted an actual distance between us, this fact did nothing to make a difference in the distance that was really between us. At all events, the idea was to stay on your toes. Anything could trigger it off—make Dad gasp. Which was especially the case with the Seven-Up that somebody must have always been encouraging Dad to sip. Namely, one of the people who probably were administering Dad's dilations. Which is to say that this is what they were called—esophageal dilations. Jesus, what a thing this sounds like to me, esophageal dilations. Anyway, it turned out that the doctor who was doing it was at Mount Sinai Hospital and that Natalie had been coming over once a week to pick Dad up and take him. By the way, I saw it once, you know. I mean, I was there and saw them give Dad one of these procedures, a dilation. After all, there was no chance of Natalie coming around with me anywhere around, this you can depend on. No, no, Natalie was not anywhere in sight that week—except, of course, after the accident. So that it just naturally fell to me to take Dad over there and be the one to be with him. So I saw one once. I saw Dad undergo one of those esophageal dilations once—which, as events had it, it turned out to be Dad's last one. Look, I may as well tell you that we went there and came back from there by taxicab—and that I did not see any necessity for me to interfere with Dad when he reached into his pocket to be the one to pay for it. Not that I did not go in with him—which I have no proof of but which I do not mind telling you that I am willing to think that maybe Natalie didn't. No, no, I do not mean just into the waiting room, just into the little waiting room with the other patients and the receptionist and so on. I mean all the way into the treatment room where Dad had to go for him to have his treatment, to be dilated, to have his esophagus dilated. Not that the nurse did not try to get me not to. It was perfectly plain to me that the receptionist and that the nurse, that they were both trying to be perfectly subtle about it, but that they were trying to make it plain to me that it was not required of me to do other than just to stay there where I was and wait for Dad in the waiting room. I have to tell you something—I wish I had. I have to tell you something—I would not hear the squeaks in my head if I had. Oh no, I certainly understood them to be warning me, that the receptionist, the nurse, were doing their best to warn me. But I could see what Dad wanted too. Or, anyhow, guessed what he did. Which is to say that it seemed to me that Dad did not want for me not to go in with him. At least I can tell you this—he certainly did nothing to stop me from doing it. Whereas I would have thought that if you are the father of somebody, you would go out of your way to keep it to yourself, your suffering. Truth to tell, I think I actually remember Dad doing something to get me to go with him—but I do not remember what it actually was. But it was like "A son should see"—even though there was never anything actually said like that, of course. Yes, yes, standing up here saying all of these things, you suddenly think you know everything, I keep feeling I know everything, that what has been forgotten, or was never even known, is suddenly revealed. You know what I say? I say that my father wanted for me to see what he could do. A lesson, let us say—for my own good. So I went with him—and went in—and to a certain extent, but to probably really only to a very slight extent, I saw. Certainly I saw enough to see that my father was never fearful. Well, he never cried out. I never heard my father cry out. I heard the squeaks, all right, but I did not hear my father make one peep, not even when they were fitting the biggest ones in. You see, they have a sort of tray affair. One of those medical-room, treatment-room, I suppose you could say, tray affairs. Stainless steel, of course. And this one, it was even up on wheels. Some sort of adjustable apparatus whereby they can roll the whole contraption over to where the patient is. And then adjust it to the head height of whoever it is. Namely, of whoever is sitting there on the stool. Which is the other thing—the stool. Dad was seated on a stool. White. Painted white. Well, most of it was—because there were places on it where the paint was chipped pretty much off. It was one of those swivel affairs—and as for Dad, well, they had Dad swiveled all the way up on it. I mean, it seemed to me that they made a special point of it, the fact that for my father they were going to have to swivel the stool all of the way up for him. Oh, it was a squalid-looking business, I can tell you. I mean, it looked dirty-looking to me. What I could see of it, I tell you, it really seemed to me that it had a shameful-looking look to it. Namely, the room, the stool, the tray of rubber things, the dilators, I suppose you say—with the nurse standing behind where Dad was sitting with a plastic smock on her over her uniform and with Dad himself sitting with a plastic smock of his own with a big bow on it in back. Dirty-looking, soiled-looking—despite everything, quite obviously, being impeccably clean. Well, they had these eight rubber-looking objects, the dilators, if this is what they are called—because I certainly do not know what else they would be called. Anyway, they had them arrayed, laid out as in an array—from size to size, that is. Because the size of them is actually graduated. The nurse stands behind you. She holds your head. They tell you to let your head go back until it reaches as far back as her hands. The nurse stands there with her hands out in front of her waiting for you to let your head back until it is resting on her hands. That is what happens first—the doctor saying for you just to relax and to let your head go back. Then he reaches over and gets a tube of jelly and gets the first dilator out of the plastic wrapping that they have it wrapped in and gives the dilator a good coating of jelly all over it and then he says, "All set, Phillie?" There are eight of them. I think I probably told you that there are eight of them. "All set, Phillie?" Tapered actually. Which made them, once he got them out of the plastic wrapping and before he got them coated with the jelly, which made them look to me like carrots. Although they were too big for anything even in make-believe like carrots. Well, they looked rubbery—but they probably weren't really. In other words, I expect that they had to be pretty firm, in fact—otherwise, I can see how it would be a problem. Even so, even with the jelly on them, when he got to the biggest ones, when the doctor did, it squeaked—I could hear squeaks. Quite obviously, they wouldn't have reached all of the way down through the esophagus unless they had really been pretty firm, don't you think? Some sort of firm sort of rubber, I think. Not that I could honestly swear to the fact of how far down each one of them had to reach, given that I really cannot say that I looked. When the doctor said, "All set, Phillie?" That was when I could tell that it would not do me any good if I kept it up and looked. When the nurse took a tighter grip on Dad's head. When I saw the nurse take a tighter grip on Dad's head. In other words, each time she did that, that was when I let my eyes go out of focus so that, no, no, you could say that I did not really look. Eight times. "All set, Phillie?" Eight. Well, you could see that they were going to get pretty big as the doctor went along. Look, what I can certainly tell you is that Dad looked pretty bad to me when it was all over. You know what my father looked like? He looked punished-looking. So old, so punished-looking. My father looked to me as if somebody had hurt him. There was nothing that I could see in my father's face any more but a sort of blank weariness in it any more. They told us to go sit for a while in the waiting room. They told Dad and me to go take some time-out for a while and take it easy for a while in the waiting room. They came with juice. The receptionist had a little refrigerator and she gave us little paper cups of juice. She asked Dad where Natalie was. She asked me where Natalie was. She said that we should just keep sitting there for a while until Dad got back his land legs again. She said that it was a pleasure and an honor for her to meet Mr. Lish's son. I have to make this statement to you—namely, that I have no recollection whatsoever of my ever having conducted a program of attempting to incite my sister by reciting "Rain, rain," and so on. On the other hand, just to underline the obvious, how in the world would anyone infer something malicious from such a little ditty as that? Heaven knows, one must be pretty determined to cook up such a farfetched interpretation as that. I see no connection between "rain" and "Lorraine." What sort of creature insists on a connection between "rain" and "Lorraine"? One would have to have had one's heart really set on it to establish some sort of taunting relation between those two realms. But this is nonsense, arguing the case when it is nowhere among my categories and has nothing to do with this romance of mine. Besides, Natalie did away with herself somewhere in the interval between Dad and Mother's passing. Oh Lord, me and dates. Well, it must have been sometime after August of 1986 and before January of 1988. Not that I noticed if there was any date for her given on her footstone. I mean, when Barbara and I and Atticus all went out to the family cemetery, this to handle the interment of Mother's cremains. Which is the word that they use to refer to them, you understand. At all events, that was, of course, in February of the same year. Yes, February—of this there can be no question, given that February is my birthday and that this was a fact that lent a certain heightening to things for me, I think I can say. So, yes, yes, they are all back up here with me now—namely, out there in the family plot where my family picked a cemetery. Right out here, in fact, on Long Island, I mean. Anyway, yes, there was a footstone there for Natalie over there on the other side of Dad's when Barbara and I and Atticus came out here to Long Island to see to the requirements concerning Mother's cremains. But if there was a date shown—I mean, apart from the spread of Natalie's years—then it certainly must have escaped my attention. Span, I mean—span is what I should have said, I think. I think that is what the expression is. Well, no one is buried in Florida. No Lishes, that is. Not that I am likely to forget anything which ensued when the three of us went out there for Mother. Oh no, nothing is ever likely to make me forget what they had in store for me when I went out there with my little family to see to the matter of taking care of things for Mother. What I mean is the package. What I am getting at is the wrapping paper on the package—or even more specifically, even more particularly, not so much just the package and the wrapping paper as the packing tape, or wrapping tape, if this is what you call it. Because I would really like to know what they call it. And with Barbara and Atticus having to stand right there with me at the service window! The crust of those people! Or whoever it is who did that—handing me something like that. The gall of them. My family standing right there with me and a thing like that making such a fool of me. Don't people ever stop to think any more? I want to know something—don't people ever stop to think any more? Well, as I was saying, it was just the one time that I went over there to Mount Sinai with Dad, whereas Natalie had theretofore been taking him. But, quite right, quite right, there was no need for anyone to go to the bother after that. My father did not have to put his head back after that for anyone any more nor thereafter open up his mouth for anyone any more, the fact being that Dad finally surrendered to his injuries before it was time for me to have to go back up to New York. As for Natalie, she took pills, it was reported to me. This is what was reported to me. The doctor who signed the death certificate was also the doctor who got in touch with me. He said it was pills. But I am asking you, was it because of Dad? Look, all I can also tell you is that she had cancers too—specifically both breasts. As concerns everything else, the woman was alone, was lonely probably—all the usuals, divorced, everything else. But I grant you that my information is not the best. It was just a telephone call. What information I used to come into possession of about my family, it was almost always by telephone and therefore never anything better, I suppose, than sketchy at best. Or did you forget that they all went down to Florida in 1962?—whereas I, for my part, went instead out to the desert to seek the much more potent sun you can get out West. Well, maybe no hotter, maybe sometimes not even as hot, but a sun which is much more astringent, I think we can say. At least that was the way it certainly felt to me when I used to sit out in it sunbathing myself in Gila Bend. Until, as I have already explained, thanks to the action of methotrexate and methoxsalen, I could come back to New York and take the job that was being offered to me as the fiction editor at *Esquire* magazine. Oh, it was great. It went off without a hitch, up on the roof there at 488 Madison Avenue as often as I could get. But what I have not thus far told you is this—it wasn't anywhere so easy as that when I had to move from *Esquire* and go to Knopf. Hence, the note I made when I made these four little notes on this little business card up here. The note not rightly written as "The Office" but wrongly written as "The Room." Because, yes, there really was a moment of very considerable alarm for me back when I first moved into my new job in the building at 201 East Fiftieth Street. No, no, it wasn't that I was worried about anything to do with employment. My God, far from it, far from it—given the fact that Bob Gottlieb at Knopf, the editor-in-chief at Knopf—namely, of the publishing house of Alfred A. Knopf—who himself—Gottlieb, I mean—who himself is, incidentally, now off being the editor-in-chief, it happens, not of another book publishing house but of a magazine—specifically *The New Yorker* magazine—anyway, given the fact that Gottlieb had hired me on at Knopf almost the very day the new people at *Esquire* had sent me on my way. So, no, it was not that there was anything about my work as such that had me in such a state. What it was—well, it was just a question of my getting a new set-up somewhere up on a new roof. Because what happened was that the highly irregular set-up I had been getting away with up on the roof of the building where *Esquire* was, nothing like it was to be forthcoming there on top of the building where Knopf was. And is. Which address—namely, 201 East Fiftieth Street—well, with as many writers as there are of you sitting out there, doubtless plenty of you know that this is the address of the Random House building. And probably just as many of you know that it also goes for Knopf, this address—given the fact that Alfred A. Knopf is a Random House imprint. Or, I don't know—division, affiliate, subsidiary. At any rate, my being able to get access to the Random House roof, this turned out to be entirely out of the question. I had had my hopes, of course—but I could tell that this was going to be a different matter altogether, such a bigger, taller building, such a much more sort of corporate building.

Whatever the obstacle, whatever the stumbling block, I was not going to be able to take my methoxsalen, put everything I needed into Barbara's tote bag—mineral oil, goggles, manuscripts, felt-tips, towel—and just hop aboard the next upward-bound elevator. I have to admit this to you—I think I was probably at my worst those weeks. I mean, I was really inconsolable—what with Barbara telling me not to worry, that she was absolutely positive that something was going to turn up, but meanwhile the psoriasis, my psoriasis, it was really, as the expression goes, on the march. Oh yes, Barbara could certainly tell you. I was beside myself. Quite obviously, yes, I had a job, but what good was a job going to do me if my skin just kept erupting and erupting until, all over again, it was in such a state that I could not think straight? Because I have not told you any of this yet—no, no, we could not possibly have the time for me to go into any of this with you yet—and besides, my vectors, the matter of governance, they wouldn't give me the room for me to—but there were times sometimes when they had to put me into insane asylums for it. So you tell me, how was I supposed to go about looking out for my little family? Because, yes, yes, we were a family by then—Barbara and I had Atticus by then. But so how was I supposed to go about looking out for everybody if my skin was in such a state that I could not even think a thought, let alone sit and read a book and then make up my mind about whether or not it was a book I liked or not? Barbara could tell you. Barbara remembers. Whatever happens, Barbara is going to remember. When it comes to memories, Barbara is the one who can really remember. How, for example, I kept worrying night after night about how in the world it was going to be possible for us to stay on in New York. Without the sun, it was out of the question, everything was going to be turned upside-down, we were going to have to pack up and leave New York. Or, to put the matter more accurately, without the light. Because you probably know by now as well as I do, with sixty milligrams of methoxsalen active in your bloodstream, the day would have to be a pretty wretched day for my skin not to get some benefit from just the light. Let me tell you, it took a lot to keep me indoors. Shirt off, trousers off, goggles and mineral oil on—it had to be pretty bitter cold—or snowing or raining—for me to give up a session outside. Oh, Barbara could tell you, make no mistake of it—I was beside myself with grief. What to do, what to do? Go pay a hospital for an ultraviolet light machine or something, go patronize a suntanning salon or something? Me, my father's son? When daylight is free? But you know how it is with a thing like this—the problem could not look more obstinate to you, but there the solution suddenly is, sitting there all of a sudden right where it is. All I had to do was look, take a look, look around the floor. In other words, Knopf's floor—the twenty-first floor. Which is to say that it only remained for me to go from office to office and take a look outside from every window to see what was what in the neighborhood. My aim namely being to spot an alternative rooftop or two. My aim namely being to see if I could spot something that was both near enough by, on the one hand, and that might also prove to be accessible to me, on the other. Oh God, no sooner said than done. For there, indeed, it was, right there from Gottlieb's very office—right out of Gottlieb's eastward-facing window—that I spotted the perfect set-up. Truly, it was deliverance. Because right down there there was the roof of a small hotel with a whole rooftop set-up for sunbathing on it. Namely, the Pickwick Hotel. Which turned out to be no farther away from the Random House building than a block and a half. Fifty-first Street between Second Avenue and Third. What luck it was.

What a piece of luck it was. Do you see what I am saying? It was all set up for it—which is to say that it had a sort of boardwalk deck that ran around over most of it and that there were chairs up there. You know those old-fashioned-looking wooden chairs? Those sort of slatted affairs? You must know what I mean. Chances are that there are probably some of them over there on the grounds across the street where I am staying tonight at—I forget the name of it—that motel. Sort of forlorn-looking affairs—that's what they had, a handful of green-painted chairs that looked like that. Slats. Adirondack chairs—my God, isn't this what they are called? Anyway, I was so thrilled. It was all so easy—and even the name—imagine it, the Pickwick Hotel. Well, I watched it for a week. I made it my business to keep my eye out for any traffic on it over the course of the lunch hour for as much as a week. And then—when I was quite sure that there would be no disruption of my privacy, when I was quite certain that at least over the course of the lunch hour the roof of the Pickwick was not likely to be used—I went the block and a half it took, cut quickly into the lobby, stepped promptly into the first elevator that came, pressed the button for the topmost floor, and then made my way along the corridor to the door that led through to a stairway that then took you up to a further door—and then I went out through that door and right out onto the roof. It was even marked for me the whole way. There were even signs up there on the fourteenth floor that said to you TO THE ROOF. There was even an arrow that courteously pointed the way. And the door, the doors, neither of them, not once in all the years that I have been using the Pickwick's roof, has ever been locked against me. So you see how wonderful it was? All I had to do was to step into the lobby with a certain businesslike-looking air about me—or, anyhow, with that businesslike-looking tote bag of Barbara's I always have at my office with me. To this day no one has ever sought to challenge me. Though, of course, those signs I remarked up there on the fourteenth floor, it will not come as any surprise to you that they also say STRICTLY FOR THE USE OF GUESTS. In any event, that first time I just told you about, it was just a test. In other words, I just wanted to see what it was really going to be like up there—see if I could get away with getting up there in the first place and then sitting for as much as an hour up there with what sort of likelihood of anybody coming up there and giving me any grief. No, truly, it could not have been a better arrangement—and compared with being up on top of the *Esquire* building, at the Pickwick it was even comfortable even—and you didn't feel as wide open in the air. It did not make you feel as out in the open, let us say, and in the air and unsafe. Oh no, it would have been the worst sort of devastation for me, being seen by someone when I was up there exposed. Yet you want to hear the craziest part of all this? This should really amaze you, the amazing irony of this. Namely, that it was via the Pickwick that it came to happen that I thereafter, at an interval of roughly every two weeks, fell into the practice of being seen sitting naked by someone. Well, I am talking about a certain someone. From time to time at intervals of, on average, I would say, of every two weeks. Since 1976. And actually in her office, that is—the two of us with our clothes off. And even more astonishing than this is is the fact that the office I am talking about—and this is the office that should have been noted here on this business card as a heading in my notes—is an office in the Random House building. Yes, yes, how can I not realize how impossible it must be, even with the strictness of my course, for all of you sitting out there to follow? But the facts are these—these are the facts. It was there on the roof of the Pickwick—the roof of the

Pickwick was where it first happened that I could see that she had me trapped, as it were—but as for these experiences with us sitting with one another naked, right from that very first time, it was always in her office. But guess where her office was. Because the answer is the Random House building. Oh, but not that we any longer meet there, the woman and I, I am sorry to be obliged to report. Or meet anywhere. For what came so abruptly and inexplicably into being in the fall of 1976 came just as abruptly, if not so inexplicably, to an end—has been at an end—ever since, I think it was, April of 1987. March, April, May. Well, you know me—no good with dates. At any rate, this was where I made my big mistake and wrote "The Room" and not "The Office." Which is to say, when I was out there sitting next to Jim Salter and was listening to Bill Roberson introduce me and was meanwhile trying to make these four notes—no, five notes, because the fifth was *My Romance.* Hey, when I get down here from this lectern, say "Lish, let's see the watch—Lish, let's see the card." Or, wait a minute, did I do it when I was on the bus, make these notes of mine? The point is this—she was just suddenly there, as if she had just materialized, the saying is, right out of thin air. Let me tell you something—nothing like this had ever happened to me before. No one had ever suddenly popped up out of nowhere and surprised me up on the roof all of those eight, or really seven really—those seven years at *Esquire.* You have to understand something—namely, that apart from my father, apart from doctors, apart from Barbara, who else had ever seen me like that? I don't mean just my psoriasis, seen just my psoriasis—but seen me sunbathing like that, with the mineral oil on all over me, with my whole body all blotched up like that, coated with oil all over it like that, the lesions blazing. It was amazing, her suddenly standing there like that, out there with me up on the Pickwick's roof like that, looking at me like that—looking at me, I have to say, in a manner that seemed to me so accepting-looking. Really, I have to tell you something—in the light, when you look at me, it's really a repugnance. On the other hand, I think it might have been even more unbelievable for me if, when she caught me like that, if I had not been sitting there with these Lotus shoes of mine on. And so it went even after we had established our extraordinary custom. By this I mean that even with us so at ease with one another that we could always sit like that naked with one another, these shoes you see of mine, they always stayed on. Just as they did that week with Dad, of course. Not that there was anyone there at the Harbor House pool to see me—see my skin or see my true size—save Dad himself, of course. Yes, well, as I have already several times indicated, there was the pool attendant somewhere in the vicinity. Which is to say, the fellow who gave out the sunning mats and the towels and so on—as I believe I must have already reported to you. So I suppose he saw. In other words, there is every reason for us to believe that the fellow could have seen if he had been making it his business to look. But the crux of the matter is this—that I could not see him seeing. Assuming, of course, that he really, in fact, was. So far as I could tell, he was always off in his little cabin affair, where he had all of his various and sundry oddments stored. Which, of course, raises the question of whether or not he saw me when I had a hold of Dad. Quite frankly, the answer is that, to this day, I frankly do not know. Nor, for that matter, do I have any idea of what sort of statement was made to the police. Because, quite obviously, they must have compelled the fellow to make one. Jesus, I have to admit it, it seems to me nothing less than incredible to me that I came out here to Southampton and am standing up here on this stage and am listening to myself and am hearing myself actually saying these things—killing my dad, killing my dad. On the other hand, it was plain to me that this was where I was heading when I got on the bus out here this afternoon. By the bye, did I ever tell you that I used to go by bus to New Jersey to sit with Arnold Gingrich at the last? He asked me to. No, he did not ask himself—it was too late for him to ask me himself—but somebody called me, telephoned me, said to me that Mr. Gingrich wanted to know if I would be willing to come out to New Jersey and sit with him and read to him—which I, of course, did. Well, we have no car, you understand. Barbara and I, I mean—we have never owned an automobile. So I took the Short Line. This was the name of the bus company that went to that part of New Jersey—it was the Short Line, I think. Isn't this interesting? Namely, that I can stand up here and not remember the name of the town but can remember the name of the bus line that got me there. Wait a minute—not Coldpoint but Coldspot, do you think? At all events, to this day I do not know what, if anything, the pool attendant saw. I mean, with respect to the content of that infinitely grotesque instant. You know, it just occurred to me—there must be every sort of insurance regulation, fire laws and the like, the endlessly parlous matter of legal liability. Which is to say, it had to be nothing less than a wonder that those fellows were able to fix it up for me—this rooftop access that I had when I was working for *Esquire* magazine. Erickson, Gingrich, sweet Harold Hayes. God, I hope I thanked them, all of them, enough for it. One thing, though, which is that he never really was listening to me, I think. Mr. Gingrich, I mean. I mean, I have the feeling—or, anyhow, had the feeling—that Mr. Gingrich was not really listening to me read. Whereas I was actually going to a great deal of effort, you know. Mind you, it was no easy task for me to finish up my work, walk from where I was on Madison Avenue all the way over to where the Port Authority is, and then, at that hour of the day—namely, when the commuters are all on their way back home—catch a bus somewhere way out to some town in New Jersey. Bear in mind, please, Barbara had a right to expect me home. Bear in mind, please, that my wife had a perfect right to expect that, after work, her husband was going to come right home. Not that I am likely to forget the cash that I had to reach into my pocket for and then go ahead and lay out for me to pay for my fare out there and back, either. In other words, it was not insignificant. The question of pettiness aside, I am telling you that it was not insignificant. But what we were talking about—our subject was the pool attendant. Well, the fact is that he certainly saw everything afterward. God knows, he came running, didn't he? Actually, in fact, he was the only one to come running—until the ambulance finally came. He called for it. The pool attendant, he was the one who came and looked and then went and made the call for the ambulance. Whereas I, very frankly, was too scared to move. Or if not too scared exactly, then at least—I don't know—too amazed. You know, I have to tell you something—namely, that I am standing here rehearsing a certain sentence in my mind and thinking no, no, it is just too lunatic to say it. But skip it—can't we all tell that this is just a light novel? To wit, I had the thought, I thought the thought, a certain thought just out of nowhere thrust itself upon me—which was that I really ought to reach my hand down and get it into Dad's wallet. Before he came back from making the call, that is. The pool attendant, I mean. In other words, why not make up the difference of what I figured I was out respecting a certain number of days regarding the use of the umbrella? Well, let's face it, I understand how thoughts come—the rogue action of just the right amino acids probably, the unbidden mischief of certain chemicals. But the fact remains that you—well, the bulk of you, anyhow, given that, yes, yes, of course, which of us has not noticed that certain ones among us have already made it their business to get up and head, not unnoisily, I might add, for the doors?—the fact nevertheless remains that the bulk of you have been sitting here with me for long enough to doubtless be considered as having earned for yourselves every dire sentence in my repertoire. To wit, I was not thinking in terms of a theft. There was nothing in this that you could call a theft. It was a question of reimbursement. It was a question of my getting back what I was out. No, no, never—it was never a question of my proposing to myself that I go ahead and steal from the pocket of a dying man. My own father, my God! But you probably do not understand yet. How could you conceivably really understand yet? Because bear in mind the sun. Bear in mind the fact that it was quite impossible for him—the heat and so on, the violence of the sun. It was August, after all. It was Florida. No, no, not quite the massive rage of Gila Bend—but it was pretty awful, I can tell you. Words cannot really paint the picture. The sky was white. So that, quite naturally, of course—Dad had to have the protection of an umbrella. As shelter—there was no question about it, an umbrella was an absolutely indispensable expense, I grant you. Not that there was a charge for it, you understand—no one is saying that anyone was actually charging for it, you understand. But the fact remains that, yes, yes, quite obviously, a tip was expected—quite obviously, it, a tip, could not be avoided. Not at least with good grace. Well, the heat was thunderous. There was no question in my mind that Dad was in no condition to take it like that—take sun like that. I don't have the words for it—I mean, to make you see it, to make you really see it—namely, how my father—it was unbelievable to me, he looked so old. All right, it goes without saying that, as far as this question went, yes, of course, it stands to reason that Mother herself, that she would have looked even more feeble to me out there than Dad did. Because let us not forget the fact that, between the two of them, it was Mother—Mother was the one of them who was the older one. But Dad, my father—it was really a preposterous risk for him to be out there in such sun with me. So that the matter of the umbrella, the whole question of the umbrella—there was no question about it. In other words, it was not a matter of frivolousness. It was not a matter of some sort of frivolity. The umbrella was an absolutely indispensable necessity—I realize this, I am not for one minute questioning this. At whatever the cost, I appreciated the necessity. However great the gratuity was going to have to be, definitely, definitely, Dad had to have the umbrella giving him the shelter that he had to have. This I understand. After all, imagine it, the apartment-house building, itself white, and the sky—it was corrosive. Then down there just the pool. Just the building—it was enormous—and then, down there at the bottom of it, just the pool. Which, by the bye, did not have any people in it, you know. My God, talk about desolate-looking. Let me tell you something—there was not even any light in it stirring. The water, I mean—to my eye, it was just as white as the building was, as the sky was, as everything was. Not that I am not providing for the corruption of the goggles, you realize. Lenses as dark as those, you pay a price for lenses as dark as those. Chairs, lounge chairs, sitting chairs—not a one of them occupied save for the two of them that Dad and I are in. But not lounge chairs—not for us. Neither one of us would have ever sat ourselves down in anything like a lounge chair. Ours were just chairs. It was the same thing in her office—they were just chairs. You know the kind. I mean, they were just ordinary, plain-looking office chairs. In any event, mine was naturally out there in the sunlight. With a towel under it, mind you. I had the tote bag, Barbara's tote bag—make no mistake of it—and don't think that there was not always a towel with me in it. My goggles in it. My mineral oil in it. Did I tell you that I had brought with me all of two thirty-two-ounce-size bottles down? Which is to say that this gives you an idea of how much mineral oil I use. So the towel is under my chair and I have my shoes on—these sweatsocks I always wear—and these shoes. Here—look—I'm stepping away from the microphone again. Socks like these, like this one here. It's called a sweatsock, I think. But I was otherwise just in my shorts, in a pair of just plain—not underwear, my God!—but ordinary shorts. Whereas Dad—as for Dad—Dad was sitting facing me—except for the fact that his chair was naturally all in shadow. Which—if you take into consideration my goggles—is really a very shadowy, please let us say, shadow. Indeed, I do not know if I have told you this yet, but the fact is that I did not just sit there like a lump on a bump all of the time—far from it. Because the fact of the matter is that I kept getting up and getting to my feet whenever it began to become apparent to me that Dad's umbrella was in need of some adjusting. At certain stages, quite obviously, it was necessary to do some adjusting. At certain stages, given the motion of things, certain adjustments of this kind are quite obviously going to be necessary. I mean, the way Dad was sitting, regular efforts had to be made to make certain that he was sitting safely in the shade. Whereas for me—in consideration of the fact that I was—I admit, by my own wish, of course, but nevertheless exposed like that—well, for me, I have to tell you, out in the open like that, it was like a pressure in the air for me—it was as if there was a beat to it, a percussion. Well, the light was stupefying. Gila Bend was one thing—but you have to give it credit, this was really Florida. Old people like that, the people who were the tenants there in a building like that—it was August. Which is to say, why would anyone think that people like that would even give the first thought to venturing out-of-doors when there was an August sun like that squashing everything like that? Jesus, I don't know—maybe the pool was boiling hot. But it was empty. Everything was empty. All of the other chairs were empty. If the pool attendant was somewhere, then this is a fact—I did not see him seeing me. Or us, I mean. Even

Mother, especially Mother—she knew enough not to throw caution to the wind like that and dare set one foot outdoors in anything like weather like that. You know what? You could hear the heat paying attention. You could hear the silence listening. Crosswords, her crossword puzzles, this is what Mother did all the time that I was there—upstairs, up there in her and Dad's apartment, with the air-conditioning going. Oh, it was a sad condition of air. Have I told you yet how cold it was? The apartment, my mother and father's apartment, it was so small and the air-conditioning, it was so queerly sort of cold—rushing everywhere, you could feel it sort of rushing at you from all angles. It was queer air. Look, I had to lay out good money for that umbrella. No, I repeat, no one had the temerity to actually levy a charge. But it was plain for me to see. Whoever he was, the fellow had, in effect, his hand out. All right, a service charge call it. I mean the plain fact is that he had to be given something. By the bye, please not for a minute to think that I, the man's son, am standing here with you this evening suggesting to you that it was not a hard thing for my father to do, come outside with me for him to be with me even if he did not actually sit with me in the sense of sitting with me in the sun. Not that I am standing here questioning the fact that my father did not love me with all of his heart. Pay attention, please. Let no one sitting in this auditorium for one instant think that my father would ever have denied me anything, regardless of the cost. If anyone knew, believe me, it was Dad who knew—namely, come what may, Gordon has to have the sun. Put it this way—this was like a blessing to me—and the more of it, the better. No, I am not saying that a tip was actually solicited. But one felt the presence of the implication. Oh no, I am not standing up here suggesting that the fellow's services were not absolutely needed, not absolutely required. Believe me, I can tell you, there was nowhere in me the kind of strength which it would take for the task of wheeling over that whole umbrella affair from where the pool attendant's little cabin was to where Dad and I had picked our chairs. Which, did I tell you, was over on the side where there was the deep end of the pool. Not that it would have made the slightest difference had we been sitting closer to where those great big umbrella affairs were all stored. No, no, I could never, not in a million years, have managed it, you understand. There was no strength in me for a thing like that, given the weight that they have to have on the other end of it as a sort of counterweight, I believe. Namely, to keep the umbrella from toppling over by being knocked over by somebody or caught up by a wind, I believe. Wind, what a thought. I tell you, there was not a breath. I keep feeling I have to remind you—because this was August, you understand. No, no, there was not a shred of strength in me for handling a task of that kind as that. All right, a dollar. I gave him a dollar. Every morning when Dad and I came out, a dollar—another dollar—even though I think it was entirely uncalled for, a sum as great as that. A wind. And who in the world could have knocked it over? Let me tell you something, the day my father got away from me and fell, a wind was as likely as snow. Truly, it suddenly occurs to me to wonder if the counterweight, if this is what it is called—if they don't just go ahead and affix it like that to the other end of the pole just so as to discourage anyone from trying to manage the umbrella for themselves. Fifty cents would have been more than adequate. For what was actually involved, it is my position that fifty cents would have been more than generous. In anyone's book. In any event, in retrospect, it does not elude my grasp that what I was probably doing was putting on a show for Dad. Going overboard like that, doubtless it was in an effort to put on a good show for

Dad. You know, his son, the editor from New York. Perhaps this is what it was—my sensitivity to the fact that Dad was probably thinking to himself that, yes, on the one hand, this fellow is a pool attendant, whereas his son, on the other hand, is an editor from New York. So I went overboard. When, in fact, it was probably much more properly my father's place to take care of the tip in the first place, given that he was the senior party, that he was the one with more money, that he was the one who was making use of the thing, that he was the party who was getting the benefit of the thing, that it was his place, his building, his status in things, his position in things, these were his surroundings, this was his residence—whereas, to put the plainest characterization on it, I was just a guest, I was just a visitor, this was not my home, not my place for anything. In any event, all right, I went a little crazy—and even gave double. But had I been in the hat business? Was I the one who had been in the hat business? I could afford no wristwatch of the kind my father wore—nor ever had any brothers to ever give such a fine thing to me. Granted, I was probably a little giddy and did what common sense would have otherwise not dictated. Or was that a wrong not? At all events, it was his part, my father's part, to have handled,

I think, the tipping. So that by the time of the mishap, I figured I was out—in the aggregate—perhaps as much as five or six dollars. Not that it had been my intention, let me say, to reach down and attempt to reimburse myself the total amount. No, no, if it had been anything at all, three dollars would have been tops, I am certain of it—there is not the remotest doubt in my mind that I would have been willing to live, tops, with three dollars tops. I mean, naturally, the man was undergoing tremendous expenses. I couldn't begin to give you an estimate of what something like a dilation like that would probably run you—your esophagus, a doctor taking all that time with you with your esophagus—but I am next to certain that it is, or that it was in 1986, nothing less than appreciable, the fee for something like that, I can tell you. Insurance, yes, there must have been coverage, yes—but does such a safeguard ever take into account everything? What do you think—just take a guess in your minds—it cost to get over there and back by taxicab? Thank God it wasn't a cancer. Thank God it was not a cancer. My father was always certain of it—namely, that it was in the cards for him just as it had already been for everybody else. Interesting. That it turned out not to be in them for him. In the cards, I mean. And I should think that we would find it especially interesting that it would end up concerning the question of strangulation. Which is to say, of Dad being on the brink of strangling, that is. Given the fact, of course, of what had happened with Uncle Charley coming running and the piece of the jelly apple stuck when Dad himself was just a tot. I have to tell you something—do you realize how it just keeps nagging at me and nagging at me even though, Jesus, this is June of 1990? What is it, the twenty-fifth? It is the twenty-fifth of June of 1990. But I have to tell you, the three dollars, the six dollars, whatever—it is still killing me that I did not do the rational thing and take advantage of my opportunity to act in such a fashion as to have effected a reimbursement. Not, on the other hand, that I cannot stand here and flatter myself as to how phenomenally ahead of the game I must be at this point, considering such a long-standing program of shopping for the savings. Just figure it out for yourself sometime, the difference it is going to run you between the Rite-Aid, on the one hand, and, on the other, a comparable bottle of Squibb's. And then go ahead and multiply it out at the rate of the substantial—no, check that—stupendous amount of mineral oil it has been my history to use. No, my principles in the matter, my practices, I am happy to tell you, they have been standing me in good stead. Which is not to say that it will matter even a farthing to us—namely, all the savings in the world stacked up as a fort against the cost of what is just up the road for us for Barbara and me ahead. Sorry for the rhyme. Saw it coming but could not get out of its way. Anyway, thank God for the Rite-Aid label. Or even, for that matter, for Swan and for Lubinol. Although I must admit it to you that I have long wished that somebody might come along and put out a brand that could somehow keep itself from getting in your eyes. Because however careful you might think you are being, take all the care you want—as the time wears on—the heat of the sun, the heat of your body, whatever the agent—it seeps down, it leaks. It comes down from up on your forehead—it gets thinned out, I think, gets mixed in with your perspiration, I think—and it just seeps down like that until it gets down in around inside of your goggles and then into your eyes and then your eyes feel as if there are blobs on them. Blobs of oil, I mean. So that, yes, yes—the lenses are already so dark on you in the first place—and then this comes along, the blobs of mineral oil come along, and it can really make you very exasperated. My God, not that the goggles are not positively mandatory, please believe. Blindness, you would be going out and inviting nothing less than blindness for you to sit there in the sun like that without your goggles on. Or have you forgotten what methoxsalen does? My God, take methoxsalen and then leave your goggles off, I tell you, it would be tantamount to your going outside out there and ripping your eyeballs out with your two bare hands. Sixty milligrams—I will have you know that sixty milligrams of methoxsalen is a pretty stiff dose. Have I told you that, in fact, they're green? Because they appear to be black. In other words, this is an indication for you of just how dark a shade of green it is, the fact they they appear to be black. But this is the tint which is advised. When they write you a prescription for the methoxsalen, this is the tint that they always advise. And please realize this, when I say black-appearing, then I also mean from the inside, from my side, too. I wonder if you have any idea of what it looks like to me to be sitting up on top of a building and to see the city like that, to see the sky like that, to see myself sitting like that. It's actually a sort of steamlike affair. Inside the goggles, I mean—the effect that is created, it is like a sort of steam, I think. Plus which, there are the blobs I mentioned—the effect that there are dark clots there. At all events, it seeps in.

There is no keeping it out. Be as fastidious as you want, you cannot keep the oil from making its way down around the goggles and getting in. So that eventually, of course, it stings. Well, it must be the perspiration that makes it sting—because I do not think that it could be the oil all by itself that makes it sting. Which explains to you the reason for the towel. In other words, you might have thought that the towel was just for, at the end of a sitting, wiping myself off—whereas, if the facts be known, I have reason to make recourse to the towel again and again. Namely, because of the leakage and the resulting urgency to do what I can to get it rubbed away as much as I can from my eyes. Listen to me—there needs to be repeated recourse to the towel! Which is interesting, given the fact that it can be a session when the day is actually cold. In other words, it is something for me to have to constantly reckon with, the nuisance the oil is always making. Because it would be wrong for you to sit out there and think that, as a nuisance, the oil is not a terrific nuisance. Because the oil is. Squinting, for instance. Up when I was on the roof at *Esquire,* or now when I go up to the one at the Pickwick now that I am at Knopf, the editing I am always doing on manuscripts, the revising, I have to do it with my eyes virtually pinched together in a squint. Plus, look at any of the manuscripts that I have worked on when I have had to be somewhere up on a roof like that—because what you will probably see, I think, is all of the places where my felt-tip hit a place where a smudge of the mineral oil had got to, the result being that you can see where the felt-tip skipped. Because I am never idle, mind you. Even she saw, even the woman saw—namely, that when I go up to a roof to get my time in the light, my hands are always occupied, my time is always spoken for, am always busy at my work, am never just sitting there without something to do. Although I must say, however, that no such policy intervened between myself and Dad. My God, not for anything would I have sat there with my attention averted from my dad. Well, to be sure, it goes without saying, I suppose, that the thought had entered my mind that it would probably even please Dad for him to see me displaying myself in the manner of the editor from New York. But, no, no, there were no manuscripts and no felt-tips with me in the tote bag. It was just the goggles, just the mineral oil, just the towel. I mean, when Dad and I came down from upstairs, that is. No, no, it was strictly a matter of us sitting there as father and son. Or, to put it another way, more than ever I was bent on the severe business of making certain no possibility of benefaction got away from me. Well, what I am getting at is this—I wanted to get all the good I could from it. Namely, when I went back up to New York—Delta, wasn't it?—I wanted to make sure I looked my best for her. All right, I wanted to do my best to look my best for her. The lesions, I mean—I wanted to just sit there with nothing in the way, no work, no book. What a thought—a wind. My God, if there was a wind anywhere, then it was upstairs in those little rooms of theirs from the air-conditioning. Quite frankly, after Dad was dead and when I went back down for perhaps as many as a couple of times to visit with Mother again, what I did was used to try to get the nurse she had—the companion, the practical nurse, I mean—I used to try to get them—because I probably did not tell you yet that there were actually three shifts of them—I used to try to talk them into at least turning it off for a little while, but would even a one of them listen to reason? On the other hand, they were all Floridians, I suppose. What I mean is that I suppose if you live like that, you get used to it—the air always in such a commotion, always troubled by such a turbulence, always a sort of stubborn fidgeting presence in it everywhere, a sort of elbowing. I tell you, it was not without a certain sense of relief that I went out the door with Dad every morning the five or six mornings that August when I killed him. Dad and I went out just as soon as we could get ourselves together—the Seven-Up, the can of Seven-Up, the straw, the drinking straw, all of my customary items of necessity in the tote bag of Barbara's that I have always had the habit, ever since I started taking the methotrexate and the methoxsalen, of always carrying with me. Dad and I went out and stayed out right from early morning right through the heat of the worst of the day. Given, of course, that it was only reasonable to come back in after a certain period of time, given that it was impossible not for me to be in mind of the fact that the longer we stayed, the longer it meant that Mother had to be without any company with her upstairs. On the other hand, thank the Lord that, old as Mother was, she could get herself so absorbed in her crossword puzzles. Because you could not possibly have any idea of how much company they were to Mother, these books after books of crossword puzzles she had. But as for Dad, he was pretty quiet. Actually, it seemed to me that Dad really did not have anything more that he really wanted any more to say. Or it may have been, it could conceivably, it seems to me, have been that Dad had the idea in his head that speech of some kind, that talk of any kind, might precipitate an attack. Bring about a shutdown of his esophagus, cause it to activate a stricture, undergo a collapse. Which raises the mystery, it seems to me, of the can of Seven-Up, the fact that Dad was constantly sipping from it. Unless, as I think I may have remarked to you, the point was the carbonation. In other words, that maybe the carbonation produced the effect of keeping the tissues from growing sluggish or something. These little prickly effects, like little tiny proddings to remind Dad not to let his esophagus go to sleep or something. I don't know. Because couldn't it, couldn't the Seven-Up, be just as well what got him to choke? Well, the fact is that how much of it did he really ever actually get into him, considering the condition of the straw? I mean, every morning when Dad and I went out, we went out with a nice fresh new brand-new crisp straw—whereas within minutes, probably even before the umbrella had been wheeled over and set up for us, Dad had the straw all mashed up flat with his gums. I have to tell you, it was really a problem for us, this straw. Not like the glass straw that Dad made it his business to use upstairs—but the paper straw, the kind he could just go ahead and mash up with his gums. Because that was the only kind that Dad would let me take with us outside, just the paper kind—even though there were a number of glass ones right there in the kitchen. Well, Dad was very faithful about it. Which is to say, the Seven-Up. No matter how late it was when I went in at night to kiss them both goodnight, there was always Dad sipping away—with a glass straw, I might add, and add not unruefully, I might also add—at his Seven-Up. Whereas as far as Mother's situation was concerned, she would always be soldiering along with her crossword puzzles with one of the little stubby eraserless pencils she used. Namely, the kind people use to score their golf cards, if you know what I mean. Mother had boxes of them. No, truly, I can tell you this, my mother could not have been better provisioned when it came to crossword puzzle books and the little stubby eraserless pencils she used to fill the crossword puzzles in with. He lay there as if clutching himself to himself. Whereas Mother, for her part, in her case she kept herself leaned back up against the headboard. Dad, on the other hand—it looked to me as if he was lying there on his bed in a sort of clutched arrangement, as if he was unwilling to relinquish himself to whatever the act of lying down might require of him. Which is to say that my father always looked to me when my father was in his bed like that as if my father were just a trifle raised up—not actually in bed, not actually at rest. But he had his can of Seven-Up never any farther away from him than his night table—and when I saw the Seven-Up like that, I never saw it with a paper straw down in it. I just always saw it with a glass straw down in it. Let me make this statement—or really ask this question really—what happened to all the mashing he seemed to constantly have to do when Dad was out with me in the sun? I mean, where was it then, where did it go? Not that I could not have made it my business to go get extra straws. I mean, before we went down in the morning, before we went anywhere near the elevator in the morning, what was it that was stopping me from getting a whole handful of more than enough extra straws when I went to get Dad's can of Seven-Up and the tote bag of Barbara's I took to Florida with me? Because now that I am standing up here, I realize, I certainly am having no trouble realizing, that there was nothing that was stopping me from stocking up on plenty of extra straws so that there would be no question about us having plenty of replacements no matter how many straws Dad chewed. Unless you could say that it irked me that Dad kept insisting on paper. Or that he would not answer me when I asked him. Or that he had to go and mash them all up with his gums in the first place. Because I kept saying things like, "Dad, what say I go in and get you a nice new fresh crisp one?" But not once, not once in all those days, did Dad once give me so much as an answer. On the other hand, how well could I really see? With the goggles on, I mean. Not to mention the steamlike effect—always sitting there with my eyes stinging and the blobs having to be constantly rubbed out of them. Perhaps mashed as it looked to me, Seven-Up could still get through it. Because there was really no seeing how inoperable the straw really might or might not be, given the very considerable unreliability, you understand, of my vision. Look, let me tell you this—I could really do with a glass of anything up here right now. Good God, did Roberson even put out any water? I don't know—perhaps I liked the drama of asking my unanswered questions. Besides, I am probably giving you the impression of my paying much more attention to this matter than was really forthcoming. For one thing, it would be a lie for me to say that the woman was not on my mind. I mean, it was really in my mind to exploit every inch of the occasion in order that I might get myself looking my best for her. Or at least my least worst for her. So I was not sitting there just with the one thing on my mind—namely, the question of the straw or of why Dad did not answer my questions. Although I cannot let you think that for even an instant I ever neglected my responsibilities. Which is to say that I kept listening for a gasp. Which is to say that I kept getting up and repositioning Dad's chair, Dad's umbrella—given the fact that, to keep my face in the sun I had to reposition, didn't I, my own chair. In other words, adjustments had to be made to keep Dad and me face to face. It was a pretty constant consideration. In other words, I was not just sitting there just thinking my thoughts. Although I will make no secret of the fact that there was a certain eagerness in me for me to speculate on the question of what it would be like for me to sit with the woman and to have her seeing me not looking quite as awful-looking as was usual. So, yes, yes, you might say that there was a certain distraction. No inattention, mind you, not for an instant—but, yes, it is only fair to admit to it, my deepest thoughts may have sometimes been sometimes elsewhere. But I listened. My ears were attuned to listening. If there was a cough, gasp, anything, nothing could have kept me from hearing it. Not that I would want you to think that shame was a feature of the experiences which the woman and I used to have with one another, the way we sat together, the way we sat there together with one another, perfectly silent with one another, perfectly at ease with one another, just doing nothing but just being naked with one another. On the contrary. Shame, the absence of shame, this was the very thing of it, I think. Which was why it was such a miracle for me, her acceptingness of me. I mean, I really mean acceptingness—not acceptance but acceptingness. I don't know. Perhaps Dad was just not listening. Perhaps he felt that he had already listened. Because I can understand this. It's how I feel even about you in your extravagant patience with me, in your forbearance—namely, haven't you all already listened? These lesions I have—I could show you just by taking a step to the side up here again and lifting up my trouser leg again. Up past the sweatsock and farther up. But make no mistake of it, I wouldn't. No, no, you will never, I can give you every assurance, catch me showing you. But I showed her. She saw everything. It made me feel good to have someone who saw everything. It was not sex, there was no sex—it was just seeing everything. It was just seeing everything and having everything be seen. This is June of 1990. How am I to know why I did anything? The fellow hands me a package like that through the service window—do you think that I can honestly tell you that I know why I did not just go ahead and hand it right back to him? Thank God for Atticus. Thank God for the strength of Atticus. I mean, imagine it, the gall to hand somebody something like that, wrapped up like that in wrapping tape like that! Whereas in the instance of Dad's cremains, no one had the crust to hand me anything like that. Which is to say that you ring the bell, you stand there at the service window, the fellow comes to the service window, the fellow slides open the service window, the fellow hands you Dad's urn, Dad's cannister—period. No fuss, no bother. Or perhaps it is a buzzer. Perhaps it is not a bell but is a buzzer. Do you know the kind of wrapping tape I mean? I mean, my God, it is unbelievably adhesive. But how adhesive it is, this is not my point—my point is the fibers that are in it. Little tiny strings like. Like little vicious cords. All through it, binding it, armoring it, these tiny little vicious indestructible cords. So that God knows what we would have done if it had not been for Atticus. Not that I am saying that it was seemly to hand me a package in the first place. Which is to say, setting aside the question of the particular species of the wrapping tape, setting the whole question of it off to one side, I should like to hear somebody explain to me why I had to be handed a package and not just the cannister itself, as I said. Unless that word sounds excessively oppressive and you prefer instead the word urn. In other words, like columbarium. I mean, talk about a word. Jesus, do you hear it? Columbarium. And not even to hand out a razor blade even—or even a pair of scissors. Ridiculous. I cannot begin to tell you of the embarrassment. Imagine it, all of us there for such an occasion and expected to tear at it with our fingers—*Cremains of Regina D. Lish, shipped by Associated Memorial Chapels, Inc., Miami Beach, Florida*—my God, my Mother. The cheek of people! Without Atticus, it would have been hopeless—my beloved Barbara as weak as she was, as weak as she is, and myself, really a small man, not a strong man, whatever I might appear to be to the contrary. Because they must have known perfectly well that we were going to have to turn right around and see to the business of the interment. In other words, they knew that we were not going to be going back into New York with it. The diggers had been delegated. The diggers were already waiting. The site had already been opened up. No, I do not have what Barbara has, I do not even know anybody who has what Barbara has—but I can hear the noise in me of running down. Oh God, our son is so strong. Have I told you that it is not all that far from where we are? From Southampton here, I mean. My family's cemetery, I mean. It is out here on Long Island not all that far away at all. Just east of here, out farther on the Montauk road. *Cremains of Regina D. Lish.* It was for Deutsch. They were always saying which side did we look like, Natalie and I—like the Lishes or like the Deutsches, like the Deutsches or like the Lishes? My sister Lorraine. I seem to be running down. Coldspot or Coldpoint, maybe Barbara knows. Yes, yes, there was nothing interfering with my just getting up and going inside. Which is to say that I scarcely had to sit there and wait for Dad's permission. But I did not do it. Well, as I said, the whole thing with me has always been the sun with me. Besides, it was entirely unnecessary for Dad to do that to the straw. Really, it makes one rather dizzy, I think, the leakage into your eyes and so on. Well, the heat was monstrous. Granted, it was exciting. Namely, the thought that she would see me more or less more presentable-looking than she had ever seen me before. Have

I told you yet that she just sort of just produced herself just out of thin air? There on the roof of the Pickwick, I mean. Wait a minute, I just thought of something—namely, the attitude I seemed to have about not moving for even an instant, do you think it might have been a kind of making up for all the sun I must have lost when I was sitting there in that little tiny living room listening to the dripping? No, I was positively paralyzed. How on earth did I ever do it, get up from there and follow her off that roof or not? I think it is a buzzer, actually. My recollection is that it is a buzzer, actually. Because I was absolutely paralyzed with fear. My God, the shock of it—someone suddenly there. I was in a daze, I think—I think that's, that a daze is, exactly the right word. I mean, I must have felt myself riveted to that Adirondack chair. But I got to my feet, didn't I? And was able to use the towel to get as much as I could of the oil off, able to get myself back into my things, able to gather together all of the items that had to go back into the tote bag, and then able to go with her then, to actually make myself move, to actually walk, back through the door—first the first door and then the second door—and then follow her on along the corridor to the elevator on the fourteenth floor. So that, quite obviously, when I saw that she was leading me right back to the Random House building, I suppose it just did not seem to me any stranger to me than any of the rest of it already did. Or had, I mean. I mean, down with her on the elevator and then out into the lobby and then out there outside onto the sidewalk with her on Fifty-first Street—and then from there with her to Third Avenue, and then back downtown a block—God, Gordon, remember, remember!—and then back into the lobby of the Random House building. You know what I say? I say that it was just acknowledged. I say that it was just an instance where things were just being acknowledged. As in a sort of recognition, you might say. I was not afraid. There was a certain featheriness in it. Have I told you that it was not out of the ordinary for me to see my father and his brothers always looking into mirrors? But not vanity, it was not because of vanity—but was because it was because of the fact that they were in the hat business together. There was a certain haste in my heart, I admit it—the sense that the sooner I made my way back up to her, the better my tan would look. Which really, quite frankly, makes not the slightest sense when you stop to think about it. When was this—October or November? Well, it was definitely 1976. She shut the door, locked the door, turned on the lights—went to one of the chairs—put her fingers to the back of it as if to steady herself and, in this manner, took off first her shoes. Jesus, the fluorescence. My lesions—when I had my own things off—in that light, I tell you, my lesions looked blue. Yes, yes, there to one side of the service window—it is a button, you press a button, it summons someone official. Yes, yes, definitely—it is definitely a buzzer. Or Hotpoint? You think it could be Hotpoint? Well, how much time did we used to spend with one another? Merest minutes probably the first time—and never very much more than just shy of about at the most no more than probably a little less than just short of a half an hour. Probably at a rate of about every two weeks on average. Averaging it out over the years, that is—namely, from 1976 until 1987, that is. But, no, never by anything resembling an arrangement. One might catch sight of the other somewhere in the building—one might suddenly see oneself being seen by the other somewhere in the building—and a sort of congruency ensued. Or didn't. In other words, it was just, in its way, perfectly plain enough, I suppose, to the both of us that this particular sighting, if this can be the expression, would or would not work out for us as a likely or not time for us to go to her office and take off our clothes and for us to sit there naked with each other. No, sorry, too many nots again. Jesus, the fluorescence, I would always sit and feel it coming down on me as if there was a cure in it. But you know what else? Did what she see look like to her as if little animals had been chewing all over me after chewing on blueberries? Light like that, it is a mistake for someone like me to let somebody see him in light like that. But she always turned it on—locked the door first and then turned on all that fluorescence. What do you think—do you think that if I had not been in just in my shorts that there would have been more traction? No, no, quite obviously, no—even less of the oil would have got itself wiped off out of the way. I tell you, I was sitting there with my ears wide open. There was no question about it, I was ready for the smallest noise. Everybody had warned me, everybody had made sure that they had warned me—a little cough perhaps, a little clearing of the throat perhaps, the tiniest little gasp. Because, don't worry, I was ready for it, I had worked it all out in my mind to be ready for it—when it came to action, it was not as if I was sitting there without a plan. I wish I could tell you what I read to him. It might be interesting to you for you to hear from me what I read to him, given the fact that so many of you sitting here tonight are making lives for yourselves as writers—or are, anyhow, trying to. I mean, considering that he was a sort of literary man—not to also mention so senior to me at *Esquire.* I mean, it would be a remarkable rounding, wouldn't it? Namely, if it had been something by some one of you. Salter, for instance. That would really be something, James Salter sitting here tonight the author of something that I once sat and read to Mr. Gingrich. Not that that actually really happened—nor that he was, to my mind, actually really listening. He dozed. He sat with me in his living room in one of those wicker wheelchairs they used to have. It was some small town or other out in New Jersey. The Short Line bus line got me there. He just nodded his head and tried to smile at me. My memory of it is this—that I kept on reading to him even after his eyes would close and even after I was almost asleep. You know what Charley did? Because it was well known what Charley did. Anybody who was anywhere near that Orange Blossom Special was well aware of what it was, when my father was suffocating from that bite he had swallowed, that my father's brother Charley did. Of a jelly apple, I mean. Although I am almost absolutely positive that there were times when I heard it was a sourball—or if not a sourball, then a peanut. Well, it had been a very long time ago. It had been back in the days of Brooklyn. They were what? Dad five or six probably—Uncle Charley maybe eleven or twelve? I tell you, I am not likely to forget how Dad kept insisting on the fact that when his brother Charley finally told God in his heart that he could not sit there and take it any more, that it would be he—Philip, not Henry or Sam—who would be the one who would suffer the most loss. Namely, because if Charley had not come along, what would ever have become of Philip? Quite obviously, I have to tell you something—it really made me think. Much, as I imagine, Atticus must have sometimes thought—your father dead before you could be his son? Skip it, there is no question in this. Where is the question in this, thinking that you are somehow not just anything which is born? There was no question in that room. None in his sitting up on an air cushion and why he put on pajamas for us. And as for her, what difference does it make what it was that she might have been getting up and going to look at inside of it for? But I have to tell you something—it still feels pretty funny to me when I stop and think where would I, Gordon, have ever been if my father's brother Charley had not been able to hold my father up. What is it that Bloom says of what birth really is? Because I am not the only one who could have dropped him when it was his brother who had gone and got him all of the way turned around and upside-down like that. Which is to say, until the piece of jelly apple fell out. Or sourball. Or peanut. Would you like to know how closely I had been listening? Let me tell you how closely I had been listening. The straw, the paper straw that he was always mashing up—from where I was sitting, I think I could even hear his gums actually doing it. No, no, I was entirely convinced of the fact that no one in his right mind was going to risk coming out in weather like that. Not a breath, not a single solitary breath—and yet, look at me up here, I was positively basking in it. He came and took a look and then he went and called the ambulance people. It was Natalie who had the job of telling Mother. Not that I myself was not completely prepared to. In any event, it appeared at first that she did not entirely grasp the meaning of it yet, given that she kept moving her finger to a certain place and counting the number of letters designated. I must have told you about the stack of them that were always kept piled up in a perfect stack there on a stool right next to her toilet. Plus on top a batch of the stingy little eraserless pencils she always had such a habit of favoring. All right, then—worse than little tiny malicious cords even—more like steel bands! Although I, quite obviously, cannot stand here and not confess to you that this betrays more than a scintilla of exaggerating. Or of exaggeration, I mean. But like you, I thrive on a pastime in writing. Ah, God, rain, rain—I beg you, I beg you, please go away. I was with her every step of the way. I held her hands for her every step of the way. Tell me, do you know what it looks like when a pair of tots take each other's hands and play ring-around-the-rosy with each other? She was ninety-three years old. The woman was ninety-three years old. And not a stitch on her. Even just for her to get to her feet, even this was more than I could bear to see, given the fact that it was how many months? The nurse, one of the nurses—she supported the view that it probably had been at least almost as much as at least a year. But I have to tell you, my mother wanted to go. Whereas the nurse, of course, kept saying that it was too late for anything like this, that it had been too long of an interval for anything as strenuous as this, just for her to stay where she was and be sensible about the bedpan and not go borrowing trouble. Look, I took my mother's hands like this. Do you see? There in the back, can you see this? Because I hope you can see this. It was as if we were going ring around the rosy, a pocket full of posy. Except that I was going backward, stepping backward, making every effort to move as carefully as I could backward—or is it backwards?—whereas she had her hands holding on so fast to me that it somehow looked to me that she could not keep up with herself, that her hands were stuck to me but that her feet were back there catching on the carpet, I mean. Well, I was the one who was there—was the one who she wanted to stay to sit with her there when we finally were able to make our way all that long unbelievable way around my father's bed and get there finally to the toilet. But you probably do not understand yet—sit with her. Because she meant sit first—the way I used to sometimes do with Atticus. The way all mothers and fathers probably sometimes do, don't they? Listen to me—you know how afraid you can sometimes be, sitting on a toilet? Anyway, it was after that—after we had got her up and got her wiped off and then walked her back to her bed and let her get back down again that she gave me this. Which object, I must tell you, I cannot look at without my wondering why Dad never took the misspelling in hand and fixed it. Because it certainly could never have been a matter of the money, you understand—even his Lish thriftiness notwithstanding. Besides, how much could it possibly have cost him, considering? Redoing the engraving, I mean. I mean, what could have been in the man's mind for him never to do anything about it? Which is to say, of course, that he actually ever, I suppose, noticed. God, it never occurred to me before—the fact that all parties might have gone to their graves thinking it was Philip. I mean, P-H-I-L-I-P and not the way it really was. Or is. And you yourselves—when I finally have figured out a way to wind all of this up—are certainly entirely invited to see for yourselves. But, really, what if I, Gordon—and not any of them—am the only one who ever noticed? Unless, of course, this is exactly what his point was. Oh, I tell you, these men were such strong men to me. Have I told you that I used to see them striding around in one another's living rooms with ladies' millinery on their heads? Actually posing there in each other's living rooms with ladies' headwear on their heads? Charley, Henry, Sam, Philip—the four of them looking into mirrors at themselves with ladies' headwear on their heads? Whichever of them saying to whoever was listening, "So what do you think of this number? What is your opinion of this number? Yes or no, will it or won't it, a little number like this, knock them dead in velour?" I have to tell you something—it was wonderful when I was one of the ones who were listening. These were men who could tell you they paid people off under the table. Tell me this—which one of you could have got me to Florida when I had to go? No, no, no—no one is ever going to know what it meant to me, still means to me, will always mean to me to have been a boy who had men like this when he was little. Listen to me—I was a boy who was afraid of things. These strong men, they were strong and they were my father and his brothers. Those days when we all sat in that little tiny living room, those men did not look to me like what they must have looked like to her. To me they looked like what I think you look like when you sit and watch a person die. No, no, I am certain of it—she was not getting up and going over to it and looking inside of it to see something. You want me to tell you what she was probably really doing? She was probably just putting her head in there to not have to breathe it for a minute the way the rest of us were. Or maybe you never smelled it when where a man has his cancer in his intestines. We were Lishes in that room.

Was he afraid to hear the squeaks? He was not afraid to hear the squeaks. It did not make him afraid for him to have to hear the squeaks. Let me tell you what I remember—I remember seeing the light when she went and threw out the water. If water was what it was. Oh, how I have always wanted to be out there all of the times that I was in there. When you have something wrong with you, isn't it different for you than it is for other people? Not that anybody is not going to get something. Even you. Not just Barbara. Honestly, you may as well know, I wanted to be noble. When or if he gasped, I mean. On the other hand, setting that particular opportunity aside, the way things are, God has me figured for other chances. Well, I wanted to save my father. I sat there thinking, "Gordon, save your father." Try it yourself sometime, out in it under the hammer of the day all day like that. Believe me, Gila Bend compared with Bal Harbour—forget it, there are no comparisons. But Barbara could tell you. Barbara used to see me when I used to come in from it—the oil all over me, the junk that used to get stuck all over me from the desert. They had just been boys in Brooklyn. Imagine it, grabbing your little brother and swinging him around until he was head over heels. I sat there thinking what a lucky thing it was that I had just had them reheeled at the shoemaker's. Well, whatever it actually was, the point was this—it would not go down and it would not come up. Look at me—do I make hats? The story stayed stuck in me—which, if you think about it, is probably why, year after year, Bill Roberson keeps on inviting me out here to Long Island out here. I try to be of use. I was trying to be of use. And the luck, think of it, of the extra clearance—in theory, could you beat it? In theory? Plus new taps? But, please believe me, I am not unalert to the fact that no few of you must be sitting out there thinking of all of the details that I, for my part, had not made it my business to. The oil, for instance—the question of slippage. Besides, what forethought had I given to the actual job of taking hold of a man? Quite obviously, you have to stop and think for a minute—the man is in a chair. I mean, imagine it, if you will, a fellow like me trying to take hold of somebody around the middle and hoist him up from a chair. Not to mention the rest of it—end over end until, presto, here comes the other end. Look, I would say that there was a certain congestion to it. Do you know the word drogue? Can't you hear it in the acoustics it has in it? In any event, I am not strong.

There would have been no question about the six dollars, or about the three dollars, if there had been no question about whether or not I was strong. Is there any water up here? Did I push a glass of it back there where I cannot see it when I put the books I brought up here down there on this shelf? Look, even if I could have seen him better, I think the fact is my eyes were probably really closed. At any rate, the ambulance people came. I sat watching Mother work her crossword puzzles that night and the next night—but when it was daylight, I have to admit it to you, I got some methoxsalen down and tried to get some sun. It was all seven cervical vertebrae. Plus the mastoid bone on this side. Can you all of you see back there, over on this side here? They said it had been pushed too much into the back of the brain. Jesus, look at the time. Yes, yes, I have to tell you, this is really some handsome timepiece I have. And very dear to me, too, I hope you all of you realize. You know, I do not remember my ever telling you how greatly I used to admire it when I would have the occasion to see it on my father's wrist. Whereas on mine, there has always been something awry with the fit. Not that this is not perfectly consistent with the various and sundry other items that you see on me here—everything slightly, or sometimes very greatly, too large-fitting for me. Mind you, it is merely a matter of my having some jeweler subtract the necessary number of links. But, no—not now, not ever, not with the budget at home now having to be what it is for the hard course they tell me is ahead. Besides, quite apart from Atticus and I having to look out for Barbara, I am still always going to be the son of the penny-pinching father I stood there with all my heart trying to get upside-down and instead, heaven help my heart, did away with. Because if you look, you will see how, almost the instant when I put it back on, it slips over onto the wrong side of my wrist. Oh, but it probably makes a kind of sense—this shirt, these trousers, the shoes, the watch. The fact is that he just took it from me and got it right out of it for us with nothing more than his own two hands. Or do you call them cremains? Hey, you know what I sometimes hear? The can of Seven-Up rolling around on that stuff—namely, whatever it is, the cement, the concrete, the stuff which pool people have to mix together to get the pitted effect of one of those aprons. Let me ask you something. Can I ask you something? Do you think that he never did anything about it as a means of teaching me some sort of a lesson? Forget it, lessons. With taps and new heels, think of the inches. And as for you in your courtesy and patience, you have my heartfelt thanks for it—and for the great gift of your silence and of your collaboration. Well, then, I expect that we have made an evening of it, haven't we? All right, watch me do this. See this tricky little goddamn clasp? Time's up, everybody. They are going to come and turn out the lights on us if we do not hurry up and get on out of here while the getting is still good. Believe me, there is nothing to want from me anymore. So what are you all of you still sitting there waiting for? Surely not for you to hear me whisper to you what her name was. No, no, no, no, why her name? Why not actually his name? Besides, look at us, all of us, Lorraines one minute, never not Natalies the next. Yes, yes, yes, yes, writers, fucking writers, fucking rewriters, fucking usurpers, fucking assassins. Skip it, names. I am sick of it, names. Me, I will see you in the lobby. And please not to refrain from coming up to me and from speaking to me if I have, as they say, piqued—or is it tweaked?—your interest. Not that I am not willing to admit to the fact that maybe for as much as an instant back there I was standing up here and was thinking up here—"Hey, Lish, it belonged to your dad—come on, skinflint, keep it."

But no, no, no—this man is a family man—first, last, and always.